Oliver Optic, Edward T. LeBlanc

All taut

Rigging the Boat

Oliver Optic, Edward T. LeBlanc

All taut
Rigging the Boat

ISBN/EAN: 9783337413262

Printed in Europe, USA, Canada, Australia, Japan

Cover: Foto ©Andreas Hilbeck / pixelio.de

More available books at **www.hansebooks.com**

ALL TAUT

OR

RIGGING THE BOAT

BY

OLIVER OPTIC

AUTHOR OF "YOUNG AMERICA ABROAD" "THE GREAT WESTERN SERIES"
"THE ARMY AND NAVY SERIES" "THE WOODVILLE SERIES" "THE
STARRY-FLAG SERIES" "THE BOAT-CLUB STORIES" "THE
ONWARD AND UPWARD SERIES" "THE YACHT-CLUB
SERIES" "THE LAKE-SHORE SERIES" "THE
RIVERDALE SERIES" "ALL ADRIFT"
"SNUG HARBOR" "SQUARE AND
COMPASSES " " STEM TO
STERN " ETC. ETC.

WITH ILLUSTRATIONS

BOSTON 1898
LEE AND SHEPARD PUBLISHERS
10 MILK STREET NEXT " THE OLD SOUTH MEETING HOUSE "

TO

My Young Friend,

FRED G. BERGER, JR.,

OF GRAND RAPIDS, MICH.,

THIS BOOK

IS AFFECTIONATELY DEDICATED.

PREFACE.

"ALL TAUT" is the fifth volume of "THE BOAT-BUILDER SERIES," which will be finished in the next book. Nearly all the characters presented, and all who take prominent parts in the story, have been introduced in the preceding volumes. The principal of the Beech Hill Industrial School entertains some doubts in regard to the principle upon which he has been conducting the institution, and brings about a partial change in its character. He is a firm believer in the utility of the school as he has organized it; and, apart from its industrial mission, he believes it may accomplish another purpose that will render it still more valuable to the community in which he resides.

The founder of the school has demonstrated to his own satisfaction, to say the least, that the institution is a practicable cure for some of the evils of American society; and he adds to it the feature of making it partly reformatory. The subjects of his new experiment in this direction are the Topovers, who have been the bad characters of the story. He finds them more tractable than he had anticipated, and the story will show with what results he applied the naval discipline of the school to them.

In spite of the rather formidable reformatory plan of Captain Gildrock, the book contains about the same amount of incident and adventure as its predecessors in the series; but they are events which forward the action of the principal, and illustrate his method of reforming bad boys. The Lily is rigged, and makes a very good record as a fast sailer on the lake.

The principal, though the actual work to be done by the students is only to rig a fore-and-aft schooner, explains to them the different kinds of vessels, classed by their rig, and fully illustrates the system by which the spars, rigging, and sails of a ship are named, so that he makes quite an easy matter of it for the boys.

The next and last volume of the series will be devoted to the sailing of boats; though, as in the other books, the subject will be amplified so as to include nautical manœuvres of larger vessels.

Dorchester, Mass., May 31, 1886.

CONTENTS.

CHAPTER X.

CHAPTER XI.

CHAPTER XII.

CHAPTER XIII.

CHAPTER XIV.

CHAPTER XV.

CHAPTER XVI.

CHAPTER XVII.

CHAPTER XVIII.

CHAPTER XIX.

CHAPTER XX.

CHAPTER XXI.

CHAPTER XXII.

CHAPTER XXIII.

CHAPTER XXIV.

CHAPTER XXV.

CHAPTER XXVI.

CHAPTER XXVII.

CHAPTER XXVIII.

CHAPTER XXIX.

CHAPTER XXX.

ALL TAUT;

OR,

RIGGING THE BOAT.

CHAPTER I.

TOM TOPOVER AND HIS RECRUITS.

"WHAT'S the use of rigging the boat, Tom Topover?" demanded Ash Burton, with no little disgust apparent in his tones and looks.

"How can you sail the boat if she isn't rigged, Ash?" retorted Tom, who had always been the leader of the "dangerous class" of boys in Genverres.

"We don't want to sail her; we can't sail her in this creek," replied Ash Burton, who seemed to be inclined to dispute the authority and reject the leadership of the Topover.

"What's the reason we can't?" asked Tom, suspending his labors upon an old stick which was to serve as a mast for the craft they were getting ready for service.

"Because there is no room up here to sail a boat. This creek is not more than ten feet wide, and the wind is blowing directly up stream. It is half a mile to Beechwater, as the fellows in the Industrial School call it. The current will carry us down with only a little steering."

"What are we going to do when we get to the little lake? We have nothing but a couple of pieces of boards for oars, and we can't do nothing rowing," argued Tom Topover.

"All we want to do in this tub is to get down to the grove, and then we shall be all right," added Ash Burton warmly.

"We are going to sail down," persisted Tom; not that he cared how the craft was propelled through the water, but because he always wanted his own way, and that his word should be law to his companions.

"You don't know how to sail her after you get her rigged," said Ash, with no little contempt in his tone.

"You do, and that's enough. When we get her into the water, your work will begin, and mine will end."

Ash Burton had recently moved to Genverres from Westport, where he had sailed in a boat a few times, and claimed to know something about the management of one. Half a dozen boys had gathered on the bank of the creek; and they were all the associates, more or less, of Tom Topover, Nim Splugger, Kidd Digfield, and boys of that stamp.

They had heard a great deal about the building of the Lily, the schooner which had been launched by the students of the Beech Hill Industrial School just before the end of the term. The people of the town had talked a great deal about it, and most of them were interested to see her rigged and sailing in the waters of the river and lake. It was well understood that the rigging of the boat was the first thing in order after the school was re-organized in the month of September.

The young ladies in Genverres, and others who had attended the launch, which had been one of the great occasions of the year, had talked with the students; and "rigging the boat" was still the subject of conversation among them. Of course the boys did more talking on this subject than all others. Tom Topover had seen the launch, and heard the subject of rigging the new craft discussed. He was inspired to do something of the same kind, and this explained his persistency in part.

It was the last week in August, and in two weeks the industrial school would be open again; but the students who went to their homes had not yet returned, and every thing was very quiet about the grounds and buildings. A few boys who had no homes, or had them in the immediate vicinity, spent a good deal of their time in the Sylph, the steam-yacht of the principal, Captain Gildrock.

Dory Dornwood had preferred to remain at home with his mother and sister, at the mansion of his uncle the captain. He made a call as often as it was decent for him to do so, at the cottage of Mr. Bristol on the bank of the creek. Miss Lily Bristol, the daughter of the engineer who lived there, was acknowledged everywhere to be a remarkably pretty girl, about Dory's own age.

Dory was a great character at the school, and

he was now the captain of the Sylph when the institution was in session. He was by no means a fighting character, though he had been in some hard battles with students and others, and his prowess possibly had something to do with his popularity in school and out.

During the vacation, the Sylph was in service a great part of the time. As she went somewhere nearly every day except Sunday, Dory had frequent occasion to go to the cottage to give the engineer his orders for the next day. His message to the father was generally coupled with an invitation to Lily and her mother to join the party.

Besides, Lily had a brother who had won distinction among the students for certain battles he had fought with Major Billcord and his son Walk. Under Dory's direction, the students had moved the cottage in which the Bristols lived, from Sandy Point to its present location; and this event, in one way and another, had led to a very close intimacy between the young captain of the Sylph and Paul Bristol, Lily's brother.

Perhaps Dory wished to see his friend very often; at any rate, he went to the cottage about every day in the week. Some of the students, and even his sister Marian, were disposed to laugh at him for his frequent visits; but Dory never admitted, even to himself, that he went to see Lily. Being quite young, it is probable that he did not understand the matter very well, and was ignorant of what it was that attracted him to the cottage.

Tom Topover and his followers had been hearing all the talk in the town, — at school, at the taverns, and in the shops, — about the doings at the Industrial School. They had been inclined to imitate, in their own way, the operations of the students on the water. They had endeavored to get into various quarrels with them, sometimes for the simple fun of bothering and annoying them, and sometimes for the purpose of getting possession of their boats.

Twice they had stolen the long barges; and once, when they were assisted by the students of the Chesterfield Collegiate Institute, they had given the owners a great deal of trouble in recovering the property of the school. It is not strange that the frequent view of so many elegant boats on the river and lake inspired them to imitate their more fortunate neighbors in the sports of the water.

Tom and his companions believed that the students and their principal were especially mean and selfish, in keeping all these elegant boats exclusively for their own use. He had done his best in trying to be civil, and even polite, in making his request, for himself and his associates, for the use of some of the boats for an hour or two. He had always been refused; for they were not competent to manage such craft, in the first place, and the principal had no fancy for indulging bad boys.

Being unable to obtain the use even of the four-oar rowboats of the institution, though it was vacation, they had constructed a flat-bottomed affair, which they called a boat, but to which no one else would have had courtesy enough to apply the term. It had been constructed under the direction of Ash Burton, who was certainly a higher grade of boy than the original Topovers; but it may be doubted if his standard of morals was any more elevated. He had been well educated so far, and was now in the high school.

The Topovers were enterprising and daring; and this fact, rather than their coarse manners and disregard of the laws of God and man, had drawn him to them. With him in tone and manners were half a dozen other boys like him, who had joined the Topovers. The old leader had been in some bad scrapes, and the people were generally sorry that he had not been convicted for his assault upon Paul Bristol, on the other side of the lake. They believed, that, in their own State, he would have been sent to a correctional institution.

The addition of boys like Ash Burton and Sam Spottwood had greatly changed the character of the original band. Hearing some of their number speak good English, had led them to improve their own language. But morally, they probably dragged down the recruits quite as much as the latter elevated them. On the whole, however, the tone of the crowd was improved.

The thing they called a boat had been built, and launched with some of the show which had attended the advent of the Lily into her destined element. The next thing in order, according to Tom's idea, was to rig her. It would not be proper to make an excursion in her, if she would float with half a dozen of them in her, — which had yet to be demonstrated, — until she had been rigged. The leader and some of the others had brought such bits of line as they could lay their hands upon, not always with a strict regard to the rights of property.

Ash Burton and Sam Spottwood did not believe in this folly, and they were disposed to rebel against the chief of the Topovers. The old sheet which Tom had brought for a sail would be as useless as a steam-engine without a propeller, in going down Beech Creek.

"If you want to rig her, go ahead, Tom," said Ash, when he had exhausted his arguments against the plan. "Sam and I will wait until you do the job."

"But I don't know how," added Tom. "I never had any thing to do with sailboats."

"Let him have his own way, Ash," suggested Sam Spottwood, in a low voice. "Help him out, and we shall get off all the sooner."

The new boat was not only to be rigged that day, but she was to convey her builders down the stream to the lake. Tom had hacked out a boom and gaff, and had set up the crooked stick which was to serve as a mast. One of the boys had to devote himself all the time to the work of baling out the leaky craft, while another was punching cotton-wool into the gaping seams, and plastering them over with putty.

The mast-hole was so large that the spar would not stand up; and Ash rigged a pair of shrouds to support it in place. The sail had already been bent on the boom and gaff in a very unnautical manner, and a few minutes served to attach it to the mast. The master rigger on this occasion was not disposed to waste any time on the rigging; and the gaff was not made to hoist and lower, but was simply tied to the top of the mast. A piece of bed-cord was fastened to the boom, to serve as the main sheet, and the craft was ready for sea.

But the calker had not yet finished his labors, and Sam Spottwood assisted him. The cotton had but a light hold on the wood, in the wideness of the seams, but the putty kept it in place. In another half-hour, the workmen declared that the boat was tight, and would keep dry, even in a heavy sea, out in the great lake. Ash Burton had some doubts on this point, but he said nothing. If they all got overboard, it would be easy enough to get out of the creek, it was so narrow.

"Is every thing all right now?" asked Tom

Topover, in a tone of authority, when the calker announced that his job was finished.

"Every thing is all right," replied Kidd Digfield, who had used the cotton and putty. "The boat is all ready."

Tom proceeded to take his place at the stern.

CHAPTER II.

THE VOYAGE OF THE THUNDERER.

"WHO is to be the captain of this craft, Tom?" asked Ash Burton, when the leader of the gang had taken his place at the post of honor.

"I am, of course," replied Tom, opening his mouth from ear to ear in a grin which was intended to express his astonishment that any one should put such a question to him.

"All right," added Ash, with a nod of his head in addition to emphasize his consent; "we will all obey your orders."

"Of course you will. In a boat there can be only one head, and others must do as the captain says," continued the self-appointed skipper.

"You are exactly right there, Tom. On board of the Sylph a fellow is not allowed to say his soul is his own; and if he disobeys the orders of his superior officer, he is shut up in the dark, or something of that sort."

"That's the right way to do it," argued Tom. "If a fellow won't mind the captain, he ought to be shut up, and kept there till he is willing to mind."

"We shall all mind," said Ash; but some of his companions could not help noticing a sort of chuckle as he spoke.

As no one said any thing more on the subject, and all seemed to agree that he should be the captain, Tom proceeded to station his ship's company in the boat. He ordered Ash to take a place beside him in the stern. There was no more than room enough for the six boys, and certainly none for as many more who had taken part in the building of the boat, but were not present at the rigging of the craft.

The Thunderer — for that was the name Tom had given her in spite of the protest of Ash and Sam, who wanted to call her the Boxer, perhaps as a compliment to the leader of the party, but more probably because she was more like a box than a boat — had her bow on the sand at the bank of the creek. Tom directed Sam Spottwood, who was in the forward part of the boat, to shove her off.

The boy addressed had a piece of board in his hand, and he obeyed the order. The clumsy craft slid off the sandbank into the water. The six stout boys in her settled her down so, that Tom began to manifest some signs of timidity; but when she had reached her bearings she did very well, and rested like a log on the water. The hills and trees on each side sheltered the creek in this place from the breeze that was blowing, and the sail hung idly from the gaff.

The boat was provided with a rudder moved by a tiller thrust into a half-inch auger-hole. It was sufficient to move the rudder, and that was all that was expected of it. Tom thought that the boat was a decided success, as she had not yet spilled them out into the creek. The current of the stream was strong enough to set the craft in motion, and she began her maiden voyage down to the little lake.

But she did not pay proper allegiance to her helm, in spite of all the twisting and jerking that Tom bestowed upon the innocent tiller, which was not at all responsible for the erratic course of the Thunderer. She bunted on the sandbars, and even poked her blunt nose into the banks as if she were hunting for muskrats.

"There is some mistake about this boat," said Tom, when he had exhausted his strength and his patience in vain attempts to bring the craft to some definite course.

"What is it, Captain Topover?" asked Ash, winking slyly to Sam in the bow.

"That's more than I know, for every thing seems to be all right about her. The rudder moves when I shift the tiller, but she don't mind it no more than a naughty boy minds his mother," replied Tom, looking over the boat in his efforts to ascertain what the matter was.

Just at that moment, the obdurate Thunderer was whirled by an eddy in the current, and thrown against a log of wood projecting from the bank. She canted over, and Kidd Digfield sprang to his feet. It looked as though the boat were going to spill them all out, but she did not: on the contrary, she rebounded from the obstacle, and went whirling on her way down the stream.

"Sit down, Kidd Digfield!" shouted Tom imperatively. "You have been in a boat enough to know better than to stand up in that fashion. No fellow is to get on his feet, whatever happens."

The skipper had learned this from the discipline of the students, with some of whom he had conversed; and he had often been near enough to their boats to learn something of the way in which they managed them.

"That's right, Captain Topover," said Ash approvingly. "A fellow that stands up without orders in such a craft as this ought to be thrown overboard."

"No matter what happens, no fellow must get on his feet," repeated Tom sternly. "It won't do."

"Suppose the thing upsets or sinks, are we to keep our seats?" asked Kidd, more to bother his commanding officer than for any other reason.

"When it comes to that, it is another thing," replied Tom, with all the dignity he could manage to muster. "Obey the orders of your captain; and when he gets on his feet, it will be time enough for you to do so."

The Thunderer continued to wander and whirl in the current and the eddies, in spite of the best skill of the skipper to prevent it. Ash Burton knew very well what the matter was, but he did not think it proper for a simple sailor to give advice or instruction to the high and mighty captain. Tom was the captain, and it devolved upon him to manage the Thunderer as he thought best.

The boat whirled entirely around sometimes, rudder or no rudder; and Tom did not know what to make of it. He had never seen a boat act so before, and he was sure that none of the school navy behaved in such an unaccountable manner. The progress of the expedition was very slow; and the skipper declared that it would take all day to get to Beechwater at this rate, to say nothing of Lake Champlain, upon whose waves they desired to navigate the Thunderer.

"I say, Sam Spottwood, just use that board of yours a little, and keep the boat from twisting about like a ram's horn," said Tom, when he could devise no other expedient for keeping the boat in a direct course.

"What am I to do with it?" asked Sam, who had some idea of what had been passing in the mind of Ash.

"When you see her whirling about, just stick

the board on the bottom, or against the bank, and push her round," added Tom.

Sam obeyed the order when the bow came near enough to the bank for him to touch it. But when he attempted to reach the bottom of the creek, the water was too deep for the length of his stick. The boat whirled again, and Tom reproved the hand forward for not preventing it.

"I can't touch bottom with this oar," replied Sam. "I can only use it when she runs into the bank."

The Thunderer was approaching the stone-quarries, and the creek was wider and deeper than where they had embarked. Tom could give no further orders to remedy the difficulty, and the craft continued to waltz on her course. When they had gone a short distance farther, a slight breeze from behind Beech Hill filled the sail. In that turn of the stream it happened to be fair, and the boat began to move more rapidly through the water.

There was no more trouble about the steering at that moment; for, as soon as she had steerage-way, there was something for the rudder to act against.

"That's the talk!" exclaimed Tom, when he saw the Thunderer behaving like a proper and obedient Thunderer. "She has got over that bad trick, and she steers like a lady now."

The craft reached the hill, and again she was left in a calm. Not a particle of breeze came to fill the sail, and she began to gyrate as she had done before. Tom was vexed; and he tried in vain to solve the mystery, while Ash chuckled at the ignorance and stupidity of the captain of the Thunderer.

Passing the Bristol cottage, which seemed to be closed up, they came into Beechwater. There was a little breeze on the lake, and the sail filled again. But the wind did not come from the same direction as before; and after the sheet — not the main sheet, but the bed-sheet doing duty as a mainsail — had filled once, it refused to fill again. It had been trimmed at random, and was not in position to profit by the light air that came to it.

Ash Burton laughed in his sleeve, and winked at Sam Spottwood. As the Thunderer had passed out of the current, or where the force of it was diffused through the whole breadth of the lake, she ceased to move at all, so far as her gallant skipper could discern.

"Are we going to stop for dinner here?" asked Ash, with another wink at Sam.

"That sail keeps flapping, and there is wind enough; but the boat don't seem to go at all," replied the perplexed commander of the Thunderer. "I wonder what's the matter with her?"

"The captain of the vessel ought to know what ails her," added Ash.

"Well, I don't know; and she won't move at all," added the skipper. "Do you know what ails her, Ash Burton?"

"I don't pretend to know any thing at all about it, and I only obey the captain's orders," answered Ash, winking again at his crony forward.

"If you want to tell me any thing about the matter, I am ready to hear you," continued the captain, nonplussed at the situation.

"I don't want to tell you a single word. I know my place better than to do such a thing. It would be nothing less than mutiny for me to presume to tell the commander of the vessel what to do."

"We will let up a little on that," added Tom, with a grin, which was his apology for receding from his position. "Can you tell me what the matter is?"

"I cannot, but I am ready to obey orders," replied Ash.

Tom Topover took hold of the main sheet, — not the bed-sheet this time, but the rope, — and pulled the boom towards him. He had done so in the process of his investigation, rather than to accomplish any movement. But the effect was the same as though he had done it on purpose.

The moment he hauled in the sail, the wind filled it, and the boat began to go ahead again. Tom was not a fool in all branches of human action, and he could not help seeing how he should keep the sail full. He made fast the sheet; and the boat continued to go ahead, till she was within a short distance of the Goldwing, Dory Dornwood's sloop-yacht.

"Run for the shore, Tom!" suddenly shouted Nim Splugger, who was seated in the middle of the craft.

"What's the matter with you, Nim?" demanded tho skipper.

"The putty and cotton is coming out of the cracks, and the boat will be full of water in about two minutes," added Nim.

"That's so!" yelled Kidd. "The water is pouring in like a mill-stream, and we shall be in the lake in a couple of minutes."

The two minutes had not elapsed when the boat was half full, and she rolled over as gently as though she had been a log.

CHAPTER III.

A QUESTION DEBATED AND SETTLED.

THE Thunderer had foundered; but not being provided with ballast she did not go to the bottom, as it is set down in poetry and prose that she should do when she fills with water. All the Topovers of the present party had been educated in the manly sports of the locality, and they could all swim. The disaster was not, therefore, a very appalling catastrophe. But they were not required to swim any great distance, and the useful art they had acquired was of more service in enabling them to retain their self-possession than for the purpose of reaching the shore.

The clumsy craft went out from under them, for it was no longer able to hold them up. As she rolled over, she filled with water to the gunwales, and emptied her living freight into the lake. But the event occurred not ten feet from the Goldwing's moorings; and while one half of the crew swam to the sloop, the other half clung to the wreck. Among the latter was Captain Topover, who possibly believed that the master should be the last to leave the ill-fated bark.

Those in the forward part of the Thunderer had gone to the yacht, as they were the nearest to it; while those in the stern did not "give up the ship," — not just then, though they did so a few moments later when they discovered that the wreck was floating towards the outlet. Ash Burton was the first to take this step, and the other two immediately followed him. There was plenty of room on board of the Goldwing for a dozen, and the shipwrecked party were not crowded.

"That's the end of the Thunderer!" exclaimed Sam Spottwood, as he shook the water from his garments, and tried to make himself as comfortable as possible. "It is lucky that she left us to shift for ourselves just here, instead of out in the middle of Lake Champlain."

"Can't we save her?" asked Tom Topover, who had been reduced by the disaster to the level of his companions.

"She isn't worth saving," replied Sam contemptuously. "She can never be made to stay on the top of the water, and I wouldn't give two cents for a boat that wants to burrow in the mud at the bottom."

"I don't think the Thunderer was a success," added Ash Burton, as he wrung out the sack coat he wore. "I shall not go into the ship-building business at present."

"But she was a good boat, and worked very well," insisted the late captain of the craft. "She sailed very well when she got the hang of it."

"Or when her skipper got the hang of it," suggested Ash.

Tom took no notice of this bit of sarcasm, and perhaps did not understand it. All the party proceeded to do what they could to get the burden of water out of their clothes. But it was a warm day in August, and they were not likely to suffer from their involuntary bath. The hot sun was rapidly restoring the garments to their former condition; and the rough crowd made light of the affair, for they were in the water half the time during the long vacation.

"We have lost our sail," said Sam Spottwood, who had no interest in the craft which was now half-way to the outlet of Beechwater.

"That's so, and we have lost all the work we put into that craft. However, I did not expect much of· such a tub, and I am not much disappointed in the result of the first cruise. But here we are, and here we are likely to remain until some one from the school comes and takes us off."

"You will have to wait a long while if you expect to be taken off," added Sam; "for all the people belonging to the place went off this morning in the Sylph, and they won't be back till night."

"It isn't ten o'clock in the forenoon yet, and they will not be back till dark, for they take their suppers on board," said Ash Burton, shrugging his shoulders at the prospect. "We shall get no dinner, and no supper, and it looks like a starving time ahead."

"You can bet I don't stay here without any dinner and without any supper," interposed Tom Topover. "If I don't get my dinner to home to-day, it will be because I get it somewhere else."

"I don't see how you are going to manage it. Do you mean to swim ashore?" asked Ash.

"I could do that if I wanted to, and so could the rest on us; but there is a better way," replied Tom, with a significant grin.

"A better way? What is it?" asked Sam.

"We ain't in the water, be we?" asked the late captain, with an expressive look at his companions, as though he desired to take the measure of them for a new enterprise.

"We be not," answered Ash, who had taken the job of correcting the leader's English, and had succeeded to a considerable extent. "We are not in the water: on the contrary, we are on board of the able and swift-sailing Goldwing; and we should be driven from her like cows from the corn if there were any of the officers of the school at home."

"Just so, but they are not at home. Most likely they are up to Whitehall or some other place at that end of the lake. Do you think I am going to stay here all day without any dinner and supper, when we might just as well use this boat as leave her alone?" demanded Tom Topover earnestly.

"It will be the safest way to let her alone," replied Ash, shaking his head. "You came very near being doomed to look through the bars of a gridiron for the next three or six months, over on the other side of the lake; and it will be well for you to keep a sharp lookout to windward, Tom."

"That was because I licked Paul Bristol," added Tom, with a grin.

"Or because you got licked by him," suggested Ash. "According to all accounts, you got the worst of it."

"I can lick Paul Bristol or Dory Dornwood out of their boots, every time," bragged Tom, who was never able to remember his defeats in the past; and both of the worthies mentioned had been too much for him. "But that ain't any thing to do with us now."

"If you should take this boat, and sail her away from her moorings, what should you call the act?" asked Ash, pinning his leader down to a point.

"I should call it taking the boat."

"Captain Gildrock would call it stealing her; and the court on this side of the lake might send you to the house of correction, or some such place, for a year or two," continued Ash Burton, carrying the point to its issue.

"We didn't come out here to steal her," protested Tom. "The captain would say we had no right to come on board of her; but you was the first one to get on board of her."

"I don't think the principal would find any fault with us for coming on board of her, after we were wrecked in the Thunderer," answered Ash.

"Of course he couldn't. That's one thing. The next is, shall we leave in the boat, or stay on board of her? We might as well drown as starve to death," argued Tom.

The high-school boy scratched his head, for there seemed to be some force in the late captain's argument. He was opposed to going without his dinner and supper, and he did not believe that a man as reasonable as Captain Gildrock would ask such a sacrifice of him. It occurred to him, that the gardener of the estate, or some of the stable-men, might be at home, and might be called to their assistance, if they shouted persistently for help. He proposed this to Tom, but it was received with a sneer.

"The boats are locked up in the new boat-house, and the gardener don't keep the keys," replied Tom. "You might as well holler for the captain himself, at Whitehall, as to try to find any one on the place when he is away."

"It couldn't do any great harm if we should sail the Goldwing up to the wharf," said Ash, as much to himself as to his companions. He did not like the idea of taking the boat, for Captain Gildrock was a Tartar to deal with in such matters.

"Of course it won't!" exclaimed Tom. "We can't do any other way. We should be fools to stay here and starve to death, within a quarter of a mile of the land."

Tom had made up his mind some time before, and had looked the boat over to ascertain whether or not she was available. During the summer the Goldwing had been supplied with a horizontal wheel, and the tiller could not be locked up in the cabin. But even if it had been, the cabin-doors were not locked as usual, for the reason that one of the crew had dropped the key over-board, and another had not been fitted. Tom found that there was nothing to prevent his party from getting the sloop under way.

Ash Burton and Sam Spottwood had always been law-abiding young men, as most of the others on board were not. If the proposition had been made on shore, to go off and take the Gold-wing for a sail, in the absence of the owner, they would not have consented to take part in such an affair. But they had been put on her deck almost in spite of themselves; they had saved themselves from possible drowning by getting on board of her, for they did not believe they could swim to the shore.

Tom Topover's argument had its influence upon them; and they finally consented to assist in taking the boat, for the purpose of reaching the shore. The moorings were cast off, and the main-sail hoisted rather by tacit consent than by actual agreement. Ash assisted in the work, or it might never have been done, for the want of knowledge how to do it on the part of the others.

"Who is to be captain of this craft?" asked Ash, when the matter came to his mind.

"I am, of course," replied Tom confidently.

"All right," added Ash, who had thought he might not feel confident to handle the sloop. "I will obey orders, and do just what you tell me."

Tom went to the wheel. He had not noticed it particularly before, and he had no more idea of its use than he had of handling a quadrant or a log-line.

"What's this thing? and where is the tiller?" asked Tom, as he gave the wheel a twirl.

Ash Burton, who was the only one who was competent to answer the question, made no reply. The boat had been got under way in the most unseamanlike manner, and she was now drifting towards the outlet. There was wind enough to make the sail bang about above the heads of the party, for it had not been trimmed to any course. Tom studied the working of the wheel for a time, for he had come to the conclusion that it was to be used instead of a tiller. He turned it as far as he could, one way, and then looked over the stern, to note the position of the rudder. Then he reversed the wheel, and looked again. He had solved the mystery, and partially got the hang of the thing.

The wind was west; and Tom pulled away at the main sheet, until, guided by his experience in the Thunderer, he filled the sail. The sloop started off at a speed that startled the skipper.

She heeled over, and frightened some of the party, who were not used to the movements of a sailboat. By feeling his way, the skipper had brought the sloop on the starboard tack, headed for the outlet. The direction was not Tom's choice; but, trimmed as she was, she would not go any other way.

Ash Burton wanted to protest against being carried away from the wharf, but he would not interfere with the skipper.

CHAPTER IV.

A MUTINY, AND A NEW SKIPPER.

ASH BURTON did not believe that Tom Topover could handle the Goldwing; and he was anxious to have him appeal to him for assistance, which, however, he had decided not to render while the present incumbent remained as captain. Tom was sailing the boat away from the wharf, and two of the party at least were strongly opposed to doing so. The wind was fair for the wharf, but Tom had not the most remote idea of the way to bring the sloop about. His nautical education had been confined to rowboats.

Ash walked forward to the forecastle, where Sam Spottwood had seated himself. He was fully resolved to give the skipper rope enough so that he could hang himself, and prove his own incompetency. There was hardly wind enough in Beechwater to upset the boat, and the emergency was to be something else that would call him to command.

"We are going away from the wharf," said Sam, when his friend seated himself by his side.

"Of course we are; I am not exactly blind. Tom don't know enough to bring the boat about, and that's what's the matter," replied Ash.

"I believe the fellow means to go off on the lake," added Sam.

"Not a bit of it! He couldn't get her down the river if he tried a week. No; he couldn't even get her through the outlet, for at the turn he will have the wind dead ahead," chuckled Ash.

Tom Topover at the helm looked as though he were supremely contented with his position. He had got the hang of the wheel so far as to be able to steer the sloop when there were no complications. By trial he found that when he pulled the spokes towards him, sitting on the weather side, it caused the bow to swing in the same direction. If he turned the wheel too much, it felt as though the boat would tip over. Turning it too much the other way, made the wind shake the sail as it was "spilled." This was the extent of the skipper's present skill in sailing a boat.

The Goldwing moved rapidly even in a light wind, and she was soon near the outlet. It looked as though Tom meant to go through, for he made no attempt to check the further progress of the sloop in this direction. Sam protested that he must not go any farther: the navigation of the outlet was difficult, and it required all Dory Dornwood's skill to carry her through with a west wind.

"Why don't you say something to him, Ash?" asked Sam, beginning to be anxious about the result of the venture.

"He is the skipper, and I don't want to inter·fere with him," replied Ash very decidedly.

"But he means to run away with the boat, and we don't agree to that," remonstrated Sam. "He don't know what to do, even if he don't intend to take a cruise on the lake; and you ought to tell him, for you are the only fellow on board that knows any thing about a sailboat. He will get us all into a scrape that we did not bargain for."

"I tell you he can't get through the outlet," replied Ash impatiently. "When he gets her aground, as you may be sure he will, all we have to do is to jump ashore and go home."

"We had no business to come down here in the boat, and I want to get out of the muddle before it gets any hotter," persisted Sam.

"You have a tongue in your head, and you know how to use it. Why don't you talk to Tom yourself?" inquired Ash.

"I don't know any thing more about a sailboat than I do about making turtle-soup," added Sam.

"That won't prevent you from telling Tom to come about and go to the wharf by the boat-house."

Sam Spottwood had not thought of this before. If he told the skipper to go back, he thought he must explain how it was to be done.

"This won't do, Tom Topover!" said he vigorously, as he walked aft through the standing-room. "We are going away from the wharf all the time, and we shall never get there at this rate."

"I suppose you don't know much about a boat, but you have to sail as the wind will let you," replied Tom in an airy manner, as though he comprehended the subject perfectly.

"I don't know any thing about a sailboat, but I think it is high time we were getting near the wharf," added Sam.

"I was just thinking so myself, and I will turn her about now," said Tom, as he cast his eyes about him like a prudent sailor before he changes the position of his vessel.

In this part of the lake the country was more open than farther up the creek, and the wind from the great lake came fresh over the lowlands at the mouth of Beaver River. As Sam spoke, the breeze freshened; and, as the boat happened to have a "good full," she heeled over till her gunwale was very near the surface of the water. This sudden jerk frightened all in the boat except Ash Burton; and the captain more than any one else, for he felt the responsibility of his position.

Tom Topover was bound to do something to counteract the pressure of the wind against the sail; and he put the helm hard up, instead of hard down as he should have done. He neglected to cast off the main sheet, which he had made fast to the cleat. The result was that the boat came as near going over as she could in that amount of wind. The skipper was so mixed up that he did not know what to do next, and he moved the wheel over the other way as soon as the boat had gybed. A moment later the Goldwing repeated

the operation, for she was not used to being han-
dled in this clumsy manner.

Tom whirled the wheel from one side to the
other, for he did not know what he was about;
and finally she was again headed into the outlet,
with her sail drawing on the starboard tack. He
could make her go as she had gone before, and
that was all he could do.

Ash Burton was used to the movements of a
boat, even when badly managed; and he was not
at all alarmed, for they were close to the shore.
He laughed at the struggles of the skipper to
set things to rights.

"I thought you were going to the wharf," said
Sam, as soon as he had recovered in some measure
from his fright. "You are headed the wrong
way."

"She won't go the other way," protested Tom.

"The wind is west, and it ought to take us
the other way as well as this," Sam objected.

"But it won't take us that way," replied Tom
sharply. "Haven't I just tried it?"

"But you don't know how to manage the
boat," protested Sam, disgusted with the conduct
of the captain.

"Who says I don't know how?" demanded Tom, who never admitted his inability to accomplish any thing he undertook to do.

"I say so, and you have proved it. I believe you mean to take us out on the lake."

"Well, what if I do? I don't believe the fellows will object to a trip on the lake in this boat," replied Tom, willing to take the clew the mutinous hand had given him.

"I object to it, and for one I won't go on any trip on the lake. You don't know how to manage the boat, and you will drown the whole of us."

"I guess I know what I am about; and if you don't dry up, Sam Spottwood, I'll bat you over the head. I am the captain of this ship, and I ain't goin' to have any feller stick his nose into my baked beans," returned the skipper angrily.

Sam was not a coward; but he had never measured his skill with Tom, and he did not care to quarrel in the boat. He went forward again, and he and Ash agreed to jump ashore as soon as they got a chance.

The boat was now fairly in the outlet of Beechwater. The course for a short distance was the same as before. The current could be felt as the lake narrowed into a stream of less than a twentieth part of its width, and the Goldwing increased her pace. The turn in the stream would bring the wind dead ahead in a moment. Tom Topover kept his eyes wide open; but he might as well have shut them tight, for he did not know where the channel was, and he could not have kept the boat in it if he had known.

It was necessary to change the course of the sloop to prevent her from running into the bank, and Tom shifted the helm to send her in the direction of the most water. The sail shook, and the boat began to swing about, as it was quite proper for her to do; but he met her with the helm too soon, not knowing any thing about his business, and the sloop lost her headway, so that she missed stays. The next moment she drifted into the shallow water, and was aground close to the bank, which was a little higher than the forecastle of the craft.

Ash Burton saw his opportunity at once, and without a word to any one he leaped upon the land. Sam Spottwood followed him without a moment's delay. The sail hung loosely from the gaff, and was slapping and banging in a manner that was trying to the nerves of the inexperienced skipper. The noise seemed to be an element of danger to him, though it was entirely harmless. He saw the two members of his crew leap ashore, and this step on their part contributed to complete his demoralization.

"What are you about, Ash Burton?" demanded Tom, as he saw his late companions seat themselves on the grass.

"About to quit that trip," replied Ash. "I have had enough of it if you are not going to the wharf as we agreed in the beginning."

"I am ready to go to the wharf, but the boat would not sail that way," the skipper explained.

"She would sail that way as well as the other; but you don't know how to handle her, and you have made a mess of the whole thing," continued the mutineer.

"Perhaps you think you can sail her up to the wharf?" added Tom, with a withering sneer.

"I know I could before she got aground."

"No, you couldn't! What's the use of talking? You couldn't do it, for no boat will go where the wind won't take 'em. I'll bet two cents against a leather cabbage you can't do it!" continued Tom, who seemed suddenly to have recovered his usual tone.

"Of course I can't now that the boat is aground, with her bottom buried in the mud."

"We can shove her out of this in two minutes, and then I will give you a chance to see what you can do," added Tom, who thought this was a good way of getting out of the scrape without confessing his own incompetency.

"All right; we will help you," replied Ash, who felt that he was gaining his point. "I will sail the boat to the wharf if you will make me captain, for I can't handle the sloop unless I have full power."

"All right; you shall be captain till we get to the wharf," replied Tom.

"Throw the painter ashore, and perhaps we can pull her off," continued Ash.

Sam and he manned the line; and while those on board pushed with the oars and boat-hook, they dragged the Goldwing into deep water, for only her bow was in the mud. Ash and Sam returned to the boat.

With an oar the new skipper swung the boat

about, and filled the sail on the port tack. Greatly to the surprise of Tom, the Goldwing started off on her new course at a lively rate, and a moment later was in the lake, and headed for the wharf.

CHAPTER V.

A QUESTION OF AUTHORITY.

THERE was no difficulty in sailing the Gold-wing up the lake, any more than there had been down the lake. Though Ash Burton had never steered with a wheel before, he had observed Tom Topover while he was at the helm, and he was soon familiar with its management. The late captain was greatly annoyed to see the sloop going along so well in the direction in which she would not go before; but Ash was too much delighted with his occupation to think of indulging in any triumphant expressions, and he said nothing. Like most boys who live near the water, he was ambitious to become a boatman, though his experience had been very limited.

"The wind is better now than it was when I had her," said Tom, after he had watched the motion of the sloop for a time. "She goes along very well now."

"The wind is exactly the same now as it was before," added Sam Spottwood, when he saw that the new skipper made no reply to this remark. "You can see the vane on Captain Gildrock's stable, and it points exactly to the west as it has all day."

"I don't care nothin' about the vane, I say the wind is better than it was when I was steering her," returned Tom rather sharply. "You could see for yourself that she wouldn't go this way when I had her."

"That was only because you did not know how to handle her, and Ash does," added Sam; and one of the original Topovers would hardly have ventured to make such a remark.

"If you say that again, I will bat you over the head, Sam Spottwood," retorted Tom, shaking his head.

"I have said it once, and that is enough," continued Sam, who had not yet been subdued by a thrashing.

"We are almost over to the wharf," interposed Ash, who wished to prevent a quarrel. "The only way to get to the grounds from the pier is through the boat-house, and the doors are all locked. I did not think of it before, but we can't land there."

"We don't want to land there or anywhere else yet a while," growled Tom, for the success of Ash in handling the sloop had reduced him to a very bad humor.

"You don't mean to use this boat any longer, do you?" asked the new skipper.

"If you can make her go, I can," answered the Topover sourly; "and I'm going to do it."

"We can land at the old wharf," continued Ash, as he looked about him without heeding the remark of the leader of the gang.

"We don't land at the old wharf or any other," added Tom. "I'm going to sail this boat for an hour or two before I go on shore."

"You can't sail her: you don't know any more about a boat than a goose!" exclaimed Sam imprudently, though he spoke the literal truth.

"Say that again, Sam Spottwood!" blustered Tom, doubling his right fist, and looking very savagely at the speaker.

"You are not deaf, and you heard what I said. It's no use for me to say it again," replied Sam.

"You dassent say it again!"

"We took this boat to get ashore in after we had been cast away, and I don't believe in using her any more than is necessary," said Sam, deeming it wise to change the subject.

"I don't let any fellow tell me that I can't handle a boat," replied Tom.

"I said it, and I shall not take it back, for it is true; and you proved it, Tom Topover," returned Sam boldly, for neither he nor Ash had ever submitted to the bullying of the bravo, though they had thus far escaped a fight.

But Tom had a feeling that either of them would fight, and he had always been obliging enough to stop short of a blow.

Ash Burton was delighted with the occupation of steering the boat, she worked so prettily; and he was sorry when she approached the landing. He had been on the point of proposing another turn around the lake, when his predecessor in office announced his determination to sail the boat himself. This put a new aspect upon the business of using a boat borrowed without leave. All his manly virtue came back to him, and he resolved not to remain any longer in the boat if Tom was to sail her.

By this time the Goldwing was not more than a hundred feet from the wharf, and it was time to decide what should be done. If he went to the wharf, the party would be no better off than on board of the sloop, for they could not get away from it without climbing over the boat-house. On the other hand, if the present skipper came about, Tom Topover would insist upon taking the helm. But the course of the yacht must be changed at once, or she would run into the wharf.

Ash Burton put the helm hard down at a venture, and without waiting to decide the main question. Things looked stormy ahead to him. The sloop promptly came up to the wind, and the boom went over in readiness for the other tack. It would not take more than a minute or two for the lively craft to reach the old wharf. Ash realized that he was still the captain, and by the consent of Tom. He headed for the landing-place he had chosen.

The wind was blowing squarely upon the old wharf, which made it very difficult for an inexperienced skipper to bring the boat alongside of it. The structure was low enough to allow the boom to swing out over it, and thus spill the sail as the craft came up to it; but the manœuvre requires skill, and the new skipper was not confident enough in his own powers to undertake it. He chose a safer way; and when he came up with the wharf, he threw the sloop up into the wind, intending to lower the sail and let her fall off till she came to the landing-place.

He called Sam Spottwood, and pointed out to him the halyards. Tom was busy about something else just then, and did not notice what the skipper was saying. At the right moment, Ash put the helm down, and when the sail began to shake, he shouted to Sam, who had returned to the forecastle.

"Let go!" was his order, and the hand addressed understood him.

The halyards were both cast off; and the sail came down, aided by Sam, with a rush.

"What are you about, Ash Burton?" demanded Tom Topover, as the canvas came down on his head, and filled him with consternation, for he thought something had broken. "What's the matter now?"

"Nothing at all," replied the skipper pleasantly. "Stand by with the boat-hook, Sam."

"What do you want with a boat-hook?" asked Tom, who had been studying the situation with a view to sailing the boat himself again.

"Fend off, Sam," added the captain. "We don't want to strike the wharf too hard: it might injure the boat."

"We don't want to strike it at all!" blustered Tom, springing to his feet, and taking in the new order of things at a glance. "Is the sail broke, that made it come down?"

"Nothing is the matter with it, so far as I know," replied Ash.

"What made it come down, then?"

"Because I ordered Sam to let go the halyards, and he did as I told him."

"You told him to let down the sail?" demanded Tom.

"Of course I did: if I hadn't, the boat might have been smashed against the wharf," Ash explained.

"What did you come near the wharf for?" growled Tom.

"Fend off, Sam," added the skipper.

By this time the Goldwing was so near that the wharf could be reached with the boat-hook, and

Sam fastened to it. He eased off the boat so that she came alongside without any crash. The sail was in the standing-room, and there was no pressure on her, so that she behaved like a lamb. Ash Burton, seeing that his mission on board was completed, went forward to join his friend and crony.

"You did this on purpose!" stormed Tom, when he realized the situation.

"Of course I did," replied Ash, with abundant good-nature, as he had carried his point.

"What did you bring us in here for? Who told you to do it?" demanded Tom.

"As I was the captain of this craft, I did not take any orders from any one. Wasn't I the skipper, with your consent, till we came to the wharf?" asked Ash.

"Didn't I say I wanted to sail her myself?"

"I don't care what you said: I was the captain, and I have brought the boat to the wharf."

It looked as though there were going to be a storm, and Ash, without hurrying himself, stepped on the wharf. He was followed by Sam, the four original Topovers remaining in the standing-room. Their leader, though no process of reason could convince him against his inclination, was nonplussed at the argument of the retiring skipper.

Just at that moment the sound of a sharp whistle came across the little lake. It was followed by a succession of shouts, and all the party looked in the direction from which the sounds came. On the opposite shore stood half a dozen boys, who proved to be the rest of the Topover gang. Some of them were among the new recruits to the group who ran together, and were inclined to think more of Ash and Sam than of the veritable leader. Others were original associates of those in the boat, though of a milder type of rascality.

"There's the rest of our fellows!" exclaimed Tom, willing to dodge the question of authority which had just come up.

"Come over here, and give us a sail!" yelled one of the party over in the grove, loud enough to be understood.

"Where are you going now, Ash?" asked Tom, in the mildest tone he could command.

"The fun for to-day is all over, and we may as well go home," replied the last skipper.

"We are going to take a little sail in this boat now that we have her, and there is plenty of fun ahead," continued Tom. "Won't you go with us?"

"You don't know how to handle the boat, and I won't go in her with you for skipper," interposed Sam Spottwood, before Ash had time to reply. "You came very near upsetting us once or twice, and I don't risk my head with you."

"I can handle the boat as well as Ash can," answered Tom, but his manner was now adapted to carrying his point. "We might as well have a sail as go home without one. Captain Gildrock is away in the Sylph, and he won't be back till dark. Before that time we will put the boat back where we found her, and no one will be the wiser for the fun we have had."

"You are more likely to leave her on the bottom of the lake than you are to put her back at her moorings," returned Sam.

Nim Splugger and Kidd Digfield then began to talk in a low tone to their leader. They had sense enough to see that Tom could not handle the boat, and very likely they feared that the prediction of Sam Spottwood would be verified.

CHAPTER VI.

A ROW ON BOARD THE GOLDWING.

"I DON'T care who is captain of the boat," said Tom Topover, after his companions had talked him into something. "Come on board again, Ash Burton, and you shall be captain."

"That's so; come back, we want you to be captain," added Kidd Digfield, who knew more than his companions about a boat, though that was saying very little.

"What do you say, Sam?" added Ash, turning to his crony.

"I don't believe in it," replied the other decidedly. "You can't depend upon Tom Topover. If you are the skipper, he will insist upon your obeying his orders as he did a little while ago."

"I will give it all up to Ash Burton," interposed Tom, who had heard a part of Sam's remarks.

Ash was strongly tempted; for if there was any one thing in the world that he liked better than any thing else, it was boating. At Westport he had sometimes sailed in the Silver Moon, and had learned a little about the management of such a craft, though he was very far from being a skilful boatman.

"Tom will get the helm, and then the boat will go to the bottom if they go out on the lake," argued Sam.

"I don't believe in using the boat, myself," replied Ash faintly; for he was sighing for the delight of holding the wheel of the Goldwing while she dashed at her lively pace over the water. He could hardly refuse the invitation of the Topovers.

"Tom don't know any thing at all about the boat, and that fact makes him reckless. In my opinion, he will sink the boat, and there will be an awful row in Genverres about this evening when the Sylph returns," continued Sam, seeing that his friend was inclined to yield.

"Ash Burton shall have the full command, and I won't interfere with him," said Tom; but the two boys on the wharf did not see the wink he gave to Nim Splugger when he uttered the gracious words.

"Some of them will be drowned," reasoned Sam.

"Then I think I ought to go with them!" exclaimed Ash, suddenly crushing his scruples. "I don't know much about a boat, but I know more than any of the rest of the fellows; and I can keep the Goldwing on the top of the water, if nothing more."

"We had better keep out of the scrape," added Sam, but more weakly than before, for he was almost as fond of sailing as his friend.

"The rest of the fellows are on the other side of the water, and we shall have to take them in. If things don't work right when we get across the lake, we can jump out of the boat again; and we shall be nearer home there than we are here," said Ash, almost vanquished by his own logic.

He wanted to go so much, that it was easy for him to persuade himself that it was his duty to do so in order to prevent Tom from drowning himself and his companions. The conflict in his mind ended by his going on board of the sloop, followed, more reluctantly, by his crony.

"I want this thing understood before I go," said Ash, as he walked aft to the standing-room. "The wind has breezed up a good deal while we have been talking about it, and it would be as easy as putting your fingers in the fire to tip the sloop over."

"We understand it well enough: you are to be captain, and all the rest of us will obey your orders — as long as we like," replied Tom impatiently, and uttering the last words so that they were heard only by Nim Splugger.

"But I want it made as clear as day that I am to handle the boat. I know enough about a sailboat to keep her right side up, and I don't want to be spilled into the lake by any fellow that don't know as much about the business as I do."

"We all agree to it," interposed Kidd Digfield. "It's no use to talk all day about it."

The last speaker knew the halyards from the boat-hook; and he proceeded to hoist the sail, assisted by Pell Sankland. Ash considered it understood that he was to be skipper till the end of the cruise, which he did not intend should last for more than an hour or two. He took his place at the wheel, and gave the necessary orders for getting the sloop under way. The fresh breeze took the sail, and in a couple of minutes she was across the lake. With the wind off the shore, he had no difficulty in making a landing at the little stage which served as a landing-place for boats from the other side.

"Where is the Thunderer, Tom?" asked Chick Penny, as he stepped on board.

"She came to grief," replied Tom. "She dropped to pieces, and tipped us all into the lake."

"That's just what I supposed she would do," replied Chick. "I wouldn't trust my old boots in her, to say nothing of my precious carcass."

Hop Cabright wanted to know how they had got hold of the Goldwing, and the story of the morning's adventures had to be told. But Ash did not wait for it to be finished. He got under way again, and stood towards the outlet. More than half of the recruits, making the whole party a dozen, were fellows like Sam and himself; and he felt more at home in the Goldwing than he had before. But five of them were original Topovers; which meant that they did not scruple to steal a boat when they got a chance, or to rob an orchard, or to break all the windows in the side of a building for simple fun.

The other seven of the party were very fond of fun, and could be easily led into mischief, though they had a better idea of the rights of property. In the dozen who filled the standing-room of the sloop were all shades of moral obliquity, from Tom Topover, who respected no person's rights except his own, up to Sam Spottwood, whose greatest failing was the weakness which did not always induce him to do what he knew was right.

The narrow limits of Beechwater did not satisfy the desire of the skipper for a sail, and he stood boldly into the outlet. Possibly, if the sloop had not been aground a little before at the first sharp turn in the stream, he would have sailed her into the mud which the current deposited there. But he was forewarned by the former accident, and he tacked before the keel touched bottom.

More by good chance than by the possession of any skill in navigating this difficult stream, Ash got the boat through the bend, and it was then plain sailing to the river. It was wide enough here to beat, and in half an hour more the Gold-wing was in the great lake. Ash enjoyed his occupation more than ever before, and he was in a state of exuberant delight.

"I guess I'll take that wheel now, Ash Burton," said Tom Topover, with a broad grin on his ugly face, when the boat was fairly out of the river.

"That wasn't the trade," replied Ash.

"I don't care whether it was the trade or not: I am going to steer now," added Tom very decidedly.

"Didn't you agree that I should be captain on this cruise?" demanded Ash, keeping down his indignation as well as he could.

"That was only to get you to come along," replied Tom, with the most barefaced effrontery. "I had a point to carry, and I carried it. Get out of my way, Ash Burton, and I will take the thing."

"You don't know how to handle the boat, and I object," interposed Sam Spottwood.

"Shut up, Sam!" said Tom, turning a savage glance at the last speaker.

"I shall not shut up! You made a fair agreement that Ash should be captain, or I would not have come," retorted Sam boldly.

"I should not either," added Ash.

"It's no use of jawing about it. I am going to steer this boat the rest of the cruise, and " —

"No, you are not! You have tried to cheat us, and we will stick to the trade we made fairly," insisted Sam.

"Shut up, Sam Spottwood, or I'll bat you over the head!" said Tom fiercely, and he turned towards Sam with his fists in fighting condition.

"You don't know how to handle a boat, and I for one won't submit to have the bargain broken," protested Sam, his blood heated up to fever temperature.

"Don't hit him, Tom!" interposed Kidd Digfield.

"Ash is captain, and he ought to steer," shouted Chick Penny from the forecastle.

"Ash must keep the wheel," added Hop Cabright; and so said several of the others.

Tom Topover looked at them, and then he was mad in good earnest. He declared that he was going to take the wheel, and he wanted any fellow that objected to step out into the standing-room, and he would "polish him off" in the twinkling of an eye.

"I object, and I shall stick to it. A trade's a trade, and I don't think any fellow has a right to back out of it," Sam responded.

Tom was furious at this remark; and he made a pass at Sam, who was seated by the side of the skipper, with his fist.

"None of that, Tom!" interposed Ash, stepping between the bully and his intended victim.

"What are you going to do about it, Ash Burton?" yelled Tom, and he aimed a blow at the skipper, which was intended to annihilate him.

Ash warded off the blow; but when another was aimed at him, he struck back. The original Topovers attempted to interfere, but the fury of Tom could brook no opposition from friend or foe. The result was a general row. The recruits to the gang took sides with Ash and Sam, and they did their best to support him; but before the affair could be decided either way, about a hogshead of water rolled into the standing-room over the washboard.

The cooling effects of this inundation were immediately perceptible. Tom had been thrown down by the skipper, and the wave had nearly drowned him. All the others were wet through, and the sloop was rolling as though she intended to do the same thing again. Ash was boatman enough to understand the situation. He had put the helm up when he was attacked, for the boat had a tendency to broach to; and she had fallen off till she presented the broad side of her mainsail to the stiff breeze.

The boat had come up headed the other way. With the water splashing about in the standing-room, the skipper came about again, and headed the sloop on her former course. The cold water had cooled off Tom, and just now he was wringing out his coat. He appeared to submit to the situation for the present. Sam desired to return, but Ash wanted to fight the battle out if it was renewed again.

The Goldwing had dipped up the water when she was off the mouth of Porter's Bay. Ash set his companions to baling out the standing-room, and with all the vessels on board, the work was soon finished. Before she was up with the point beyond the bay, the sun had dried the floor and seats, and she was the cleaner for her bath.

"Boat ahoy!" shouted some one from the point, which was covered with trees.

A glance in the direction from which the hail came informed the boys that there was a picnic on the point.

CHAPTER VII.

AN UNEXPECTED APPEARANCE.

"ON shore!" replied Ash Burton, to the hail.

"We should like to hire your boat for a while: can we do it if we pay well for her?" continued the speaker on the point.

"She is not to let," replied the skipper.

"We will give you two dollars an hour for her, with the person to manage her," continued the gentleman on the shore.

"We have to go home to dinner pretty soon," added Ash.

"We will give you all a dinner into the bargain," persisted the stranger.

"Take him up!" said Tom Topover very decidedly.

"Take him up!" repeated several others.

"We shall get home too late for dinner."

"We have no business to let her," added Sam Spottwood earnestly.

"We have just as much right to let her as we have to use her at all," added Ash. "Two dollars an hour is a big price."

The last speaker became less earnest when he saw that his friend was inclined to favor the proposition. Doubtless the promise of the dinner was quite as tempting as the money that was offered, though not one of the crew of the Gold-wing did not think himself rich when he had a dime.

"Will you all stay on shore while I take the party out?" asked Ash Burton, turning to his companions, when his crony weakened.

The party replied in the affirmative to the question, not even Tom Topover making any objection to the plan. Ash ran for a small staging which answered for a wharf, and the Topovers all went on shore peaceably. The picnickers were having a grand time; for they had music and dancing, and there seemed to be at least a hundred of them. Farther back from the lake were half a dozen long furniture-wagons and other vehicles, while a great number of horses were picketed near them. It was evident that the party had come from some distance back in the country, and were not likely to know any thing about the ownership of the Goldwing.

About a dozen ladies and only two gentlemen were embarked in the boat, and Ash got under way. There was just breeze enough to make it lively and pleasant sailing. The sea was regular and moderate, so that there was nothing to call for any extra skill on the part of the skipper. The wind being west, he ran down the lake as far as Split Rock, and then returned. He did not get her best speed out of the sloop, and by the time he reached the wharf the hour had expired.

The party were landed; and Ash supposed the contract had been completed, especially as the gentleman in charge handed him four half-dollars, of which he seemed to have an abundant supply. But the excursionists were hardly on shore before another gentleman appeared, followed by a dozen more ladies, and took the boat for another trip.

Ash did not object, and he was gone the same time with the second party. On his return to the wharf he found another party ready for him, with the Topovers assembled on the wharf. The gentleman who had paid him before gave him four more half-dollars, and he spoke for the boat for the third trip.

Ash mildly suggested that he had had no dinner. Though he had for the last two hours been the undisputed skipper of the Goldwing, he had not ye become so ethereal as to lose his boyish tendency to be hungry. The gentleman said they were in no hurry, and they would wait for the skipper to take his dinner.

"I'll take this party out, Ash Burton," interposed Tom Topover, with cheek enough to fit out a lightning-rod agent. "You can get your dinner while I am gone."

"That won't do," replied Ash, in the mildest of tones.

"What's the reason it won't do?" demanded Tom, beginning to bluster. "I can handle the boat as well as you can."

"You don't know any thing at all about a sailboat," added Sam Spottwood, more for the benefit of the gentleman in charge of the party than to irritate Tom.

"Say that again, and I'll knock you into the middle of last week," bullied Tom. "I am going with this party, and Ash can get his dinner."

"We prefer the one who has managed the boat before," interposed the gentleman, who measured Tom at a glance.

"I didn't nearly tip the boat over, and fill her half full of water, as Ash Burton did," added Tom.

"It was you that made the row, so that the captain had to leave the wheel," retorted Sam, who did not seem to scare at all at the bluster of the leader.

"I am going to sail this party, or the boat don't go again," said Tom decidedly.

"No, you are not, for Ash is the skipper, and we all agreed to obey his orders," added Sam, retiring from the wharf in order to make room for the ladies.

The rest of the party, with the exception of Tom, had done this before; and he followed Sam. The gentleman began to assist the ladies to their seats in the standing-room, for he thought the skipper could settle the dispute.

"What's the reason I'm not going to sail that

party if I want to?" demanded Tom, following up Sam Spottwood.

"Because you don't know how to manage the boat, and I don't believe they would go with you," replied Sam fearlessly.

This was too much for Tom; and he made a pass at Sam with his fist, which the latter parried, and saved himself from harm.

"None of that here!" shouted several of the Topovers.

"Sam Spottwood thinks he is my boss, and I will show him what he is and what I am," continued Tom, rushing upon the plain-spoken boy.

Sam did not run: he hit back, and after a brief struggle the bruiser went over on his back. He jumped up, and began to declare that Sam did not fight fair; when the other Topovers crowded around him, and prevented him from renewing the battle if he was disposed to do so, though it generally was the case with him, that he did not follow up a contest when the other party "meant business." The others talked to him of the impropriety of getting up a quarrel in the presence of the ladies.

"I don't care nothing about that," replied Tom;

and he rushed back to the wharf, where the gentleman was just going on board of the sloop. "Stop, Ash Burton! I tell you I'm going to sail the boat this time."

"Stop where you are, young man," interposed the gentleman, as he took Tom by the collar. "You want to make a row; if you don't get out of the way, I will duck you in the lake."

"Let me alone!" howled Tom, as the man hurled him away.

Ash shoved off the bow of the Goldwing, and the gentleman stepped on board as the stern swung in. Ash was disgusted with the conduct of the leader of the Topovers, and he decided then and there to have nothing to do with him after that time. He sailed the party for the hour, though he did it on a growling stomach. On his return, he received four more half-dollars, making twelve in all which his pocket now contained. His employer conducted him to the tables, and he proceeded to partake of the collation.

While he was thus pleasantly occupied, the rest of the Topovers, seeing the return of the sloop, hastened to the wharf. No other party wished to sail, and Tom proposed that they should start on their way back to Beechwater. The others were ready, and most of them seated themselves in the standing-room.

"Ash Burton is the captain, and he is at his dinner," said Sam Spottwood.

"We can get along without him," replied Tom with a coarse grin. "I am going to sail the boat back."

At these words Chick Penny and Hop Cabright jumped on the wharf again, declaring they would not go in the boat if Tom was to be the skipper. The bruiser insisted on his point, and that the boat should leave at once. Then Con Binker and Syl Peckman followed the example of Chick and Hop. Even Kidd Digfield and Nim Splugger had some doubts about trusting themselves with Tom, and they began to reason with him. There was no reason in him, and in spite of them he shoved off the boat. Taking the wind on the starboard tack, the usurping skipper headed the sloop to the southward. Tom had his own way this time.

"Hold on, Tom!" shouted Pell Sankland. "Ash Burton has all the money he has taken for the boat. Is he to have the whole of it?"

"Six dollars," added Nim Splugger. "He ought to make a divvy."

"He is not going to keep the whole of it anyhow," said Kidd Digfield.

"There he is, coming down to the wharf," continued Pell. "We have as much right to some of the money as he has. The boat don't belong to him."

"We can get it out of him the next time we see him," said Tom, who did not like the idea of returning to the shore, for he was afraid of losing his position at the wheel.

"He will spend it all, and I won't trust him," replied Pell.

The original Topovers were in a majority of the present crew, and perhaps Tom was tempted by the prospect of putting some money in his pocket. At any rate, he attempted to put the boat about. The sloop was far enough out from behind the point to feel the force of the wind. If there was any wrong way to take, Tom Topover always took it; and he put the helm up instead of down. The effect was to gybe the boat, and nearly upset her. However, she did not ship any water this time, but Tom was bewildered by the behavior of the boat. She was about two hundred feet from the shore.

"There comes the Sylph!" shouted Nim Splugger, as the sharp bow of the steam-yacht appeared beyond Porter's Bay.

This cry filled the Topovers with consternation. They realized that Tom at the wheel was utterly powerless to get them out of the scrape, and it looked as though he would tip them over before he got the boat under way again. The Sylph seldom if ever returned from her excursions in the summer till night, and she was not expected at three o'clock in the afternoon.

"Start her up, Tom!" yelled Kidd, almost frantic at the idea of being caught in possession of the Goldwing by the yacht's people.

"She don't behave right," replied Tom, who had made several attempts to get the boat under way.

"Run her ashore, and let us get out of the way."

"I tell you she won't start for me," added Tom, as the boom banged over from one side to the other as it had done half a dozen times before.

It was clear enough to the culprits, that the

captain of the Sylph, who was also the owner of the Goldwing, had recognized the craft; for the steamer was headed directly for the point. If she were going down the lake, she would have headed for the other side of Diamond Island.

At last, by some accident, Tom got the sail filled, and the boat under way; but she had caught the wind on the starboard tack, upon which it was not possible to reach the nearest land. The Topovers growled and yelled to Tom that he was going the wrong way. The bungling skipper put the helm down; but he met her too soon, and she missed stays. The Sylph was close aboard of her, and placed herself between the yacht and the shore.

CHAPTER VIII.

A STARTLING EVENT ON THE ROAD.

WHEN the Sylph had secured a position between the Goldwing and the shore, so that the party on board of the latter could not escape, she stopped her screw, and backed until she rested motionless on the water. The appearance of the steamer so near the point created a sensation in the picnic-party, and the whole crowd on the shore hastened to the water-side.

Before the steamer lost her headway, her starboard quarter-boat was dropping into the water. The yacht was not heavily manned, as she was when the school was in session, and there were not hands enough on board for any brilliant manœuvres. Captain Gildrock, Bates, the old quartermaster, Paul Bristol, and Oscar Chester got into the boat, and pulled to the Goldwing. Dory Dornwood and Mr. Bristol, the acting engineer, remained on board with the ladies to take charge of the steamer.

When Tom Topover and his companions saw the boat approaching them, they abandoned all hope of escape, and gave up in despair. They wished they were ashore, with those who had been left.

"What are you doing with this sloop?" demanded Captain Gildrock sternly, when the quarter-boat came alongside of the Goldwing.

"I can't do any thing with her," replied Tom.

"You have stolen her, as you have tried to do before," added the principal; "and we will make short work with you."

Paul Bristol was directed to take the painter of the sloop on board, and the Goldwing was towed to the Sylph. The six culprits on board of her were ordered to the deck, and they knew Captain Gildrock well enough not to disobey him. The quarter-boat was hoisted up to the davits; and the yacht came about and stood away from the shore without communicating with the picnic-party. She headed up the lake, and in a few minutes disappeared in the river.

Ash Burton and his companions observed the

proceedings of the people of the yacht with almost as much consternation as though they had been captured with their late associates. They could hardly hope to escape the consequences of their conduct, for Tom and the rest of the Top-overs would be sure to betray them. They looked upon it as a bad scrape; for the principal of the Beech Hill Industrial School was one who obeyed the laws, and went to them for redress when he was injured instead of administering justice on his own account.

Sam Spottwood was sorry he had not followed his own impulse to do right, instead of allowing himself to be led into error by his friend. But he did not reproach Ash, for he felt that he was the victim of his own weakness. The whole six of them were quite as repentant as the half-dozen who had been captured in the sloop. No doubt they made big resolutions, which are good things to make if they are only remembered in the hour of temptation.

The picnic-party seemed to be very much as-tonished at the proceedings of the people on board of the yacht, which was now approaching the river with the sloop in tow. Ash saw that they wanted some explanation; and when he saw the gentleman who had paid him the dozen half-dollars, he felt that he had business elsewhere. He beat a hasty retreat, followed by his companions. He did not care to appear before his late passengers as a culprit, and he was not inclined to tell any lies about the matter.

"We are in for it now," said Hop Cabright, as they walked with hasty steps away from the point, in the direction of the road to Genverres.

"No doubt of that," replied Sam Spottwood. "It is a bad scrape, and the worst of it is being associated with such fellows as Tom Topover."

"As Captain Gildrock did not catch us in the boat, perhaps he will not meddle with us," suggested Syl Peckman.

"Those fellows will blow on us, after all that happened this afternoon," added Chick Penny.

"Of course they will, and we are just as guilty as they are," added Sam Spottwood. "You don't catch me having any thing to do with Tom Topover, and the fellows like him again: they are a hard crowd."

"We never did any thing very bad with them before," said Ash Burton. "I am sure we have done something towards making them better fellows, for we have tried to improve their manners and their morals."

"I don't think they are much better, though I know of three or four instances where we have prevented them from stealing. But we ought to have prevented them from using the Goldwing, instead of taking part with them in the wrong," said Sam.

"You know how it happened, and how we were led into it," pleaded Ash. "We were wrecked, and out in the middle of Beechwater, without any way to get ashore except in the sloop."

"I understand all about that; but we were weak to get into the boat again after we got ashore," argued Sam.

"I don't believe I should have done so if it had not been to convince Tom Topover that the boat could be sailed either way. It is all up with us now, and we must take the consequences, whatever they may be."

"Do you suppose the captain will prosecute us?" asked Sam.

"Probably he will, though he may let up on us when he finds that we did not go out to the sloop with the intention of taking her. The Topovers have tried to steal the boats before, and he may think it is necessary in order to protect himself from them," replied Ash.

"I hope he won't; for the penalty will be a fine, I suppose, and my father will have to pay it," added Sam very gloomily. "He is not able to pay it, for he has not had work half the time this summer. He would have taken me out of school if he could have found any thing for me to do that would pay for my board and clothes."

"My father is no better off, for he had been out of work so long over at Westport that he came over here, hoping to do better; but he has not, and he finds it hard work to get enough to live on. But what am I to do with this money? I have six dollars in my pocket, which I intended to divide among the fellows."

"That would be half a dollar apiece; but the fellows that went off in the boat without us don't deserve any of it," said Hop Cabright.

"I shall not use any of that money, or touch it," interposed Sam Spottwood. "It belongs to Dory Dornwood if it belongs to anybody, for he is the owner of the Goldwing."

"I should like some of the money well enough to give to my father, but I feel just as though I had stolen it," continued Ash.

"I don't think it belongs to us, at any rate," repeated Sam.

"But I don't want to keep it. I don't like the feeling of it in my pocket."

By this time they had reached the road; and they were a sorry set, for all of them had consciences, and such boys always feel worse when they have done wrong than when they have been without their dinner and supper. They continued to talk over the subject, trying to agree upon what they should do. Sam insisted that they should call upon Captain Gildrock, confess their error, and throw themselves upon his mercy, with the statement that their fathers were too poor to pay any fines. They would tender the money to him for Dory Dornwood, and promise never to take anybody's boat again, and to withdraw entirely from the association with such boys as Tom Topover.

There was scarcely a house in this part of the town; but they soon came in sight of a small cottage, which deserved no better name than a hovel.

They had been eating cold ham and sweet cake, and they were quite thirsty after their long walk; for it was all of two miles from the point to the town. They could get a drink there, for they saw the well-curb between the hovel and the road.

Before they could reach it, they heard a succession of screams so shrill that they seemed to pierce through the drums of their ears. They were not sounds made by adult persons, but by children, and they were most agonizing. Ash Burton, without making any remark, broke into a run for the house, from which the cries appeared to come.

"Pell Sankland lives in that house," said Chick Penny, when they started. "His mother goes out washing when she can get any work in that line."

But Ash did not care who lived there, and he continued to run without making any reply. As they came a little nearer, they saw smoke coming out of one of the front windows, and it was apparent that the hovel was on fire. Ash struggled to increase his speed, and was the first to reach the front door of the house. He attempted to open it and found that it was locked or otherwise fastened so that he could not get in. Before he had done trying to effect an entrance, his companions came up.

"The door is locked! Run for the back door! There are children in the house, and they will be smothered in the smoke if we don't do something quick," gasped Ash, out of breath with his efforts.

They reached the back door, and that also was fastened. The woodpile, what there was of it, was close to this entrance. Of the half-dozen sticks that remained, there was one at least six inches in diameter. Ash and Sam seized this, and butted with it a few times against the back door. It was an ill-fitting and poorly constructed affair, like all the rest of the house, and it readily yielded to the vigorous blows of the assailants.

Ash rushed into the house, and made his way to the front room, where he had seen the smoke issuing from the window. There he found a child of seven, with another not more than four. The older was a girl, and her dress was on fire, as was the side of the room nearest to the fireplace, for there was no stove. Sam and the others were close behind him, and discovered the terrible peril of the child almost as soon as he did.

"Lay her down on the floor!" shouted Ash, as he sprang to the bed in the room.

He took the comforter from it, for he found no blanket, and rushed to the child. He was wrapping the girl in it when he saw that the flames had caught in the cotton which projected from the ragged holes in it. It began to blaze, and he cast it aside. A piece of old carpet was spread before the fire, and he hastened to wrap the child in that. It was too small to cover the sufferer; but Ash and Sam fought the fire with their hands, and in a moment had extinguished the flame.

Hop Cabright brought a bucket of water he found in the back room, and the contents were poured over the child. The smaller child's clothes had not taken fire, and she was not injured. But both of them continued to scream even after the fire on the older was extinguished.

"Don't cry any more, little girl," said Ash, in a tender tone, as he proceeded to look at her and see how much she was burned.

"The house is on fire, Ash, and we must put it out!" cried Sam, as he took the smaller child, and rushed out doors with it.

Ash followed him, with the girl still screaming

"'LAY HER DOWN ON THE FLOOR!' SHOUTED ASH."—PAGE 98.

from pain and terror both. The well was on the front of the house, and they found no more water drawn. Each of the six boys seized whatever vessel he could find, and rushed to the well. They returned to the room where the fire was, with all the water they could carry. But the whole side of the room was in a blaze, and the case looked hopeless.

CHAPTER IX.

LOOKING FOR A SETTLEMENT.

LYING on the floor near the fireplace was a kerosene-lamp, the glass shade of which was broken. The fire had started at this part of the room; and it was evident that the little girl had lighted the lamp, and dropped it upon the hearth. Doubtless she had tried to put out the fire, and the flame had communicated with her dress.

The ceiling of the room was plastered, but the walls were cased with pine. With this combustible material to supply it, the fire had rapidly crept to the ceiling, and penetrated the attic above. Ash Burton saw that it was useless to pour water on the flame below while the fire was rapidly ascending to the roof. With a bucket of water he led the way up-stairs, and found the fire just coming through the floor.

He turned the water very carefully into the

hole which the fire had made, though he was very nearly suffocated by the smoke that filled the attic. The effect was immediately visible: the flame was checked, though the smoke continued to pour out of the opening. Taking the water brought by his companions, he used it to the best advantage. Their work appeared to be accomplished in this part of the house, and Ash sent part of the boys down to dash water on the burning boards in the room where they had found the children.

For some time the boys watched and worked, pouring on water whenever they found any signs of fire.

The flames had destroyed the wall by the side of the fireplace, and made a considerable opening into the attic. The smoke had been very trying to the young firemen, for the rooms were filled with it. When Syl Peckman opened one of the windows, Ash instantly closed it; for he knew that the draught of air would feed the flame with the element it needed to increase its force. They worked as long as they could find any vestige of fire.

They had broken in the front door so that

they could the more readily get the water where it was needed; but after he went up stairs, Ash did not come down till the fire was out. The others had a little relief from the smoke when they went out for water; but he remained in the attic to pour on the water, and he suffered much more than his companions. His eyes rained tears, and they were red and swollen. All of them attended to these important organs as soon as they found the time, and washed them thoroughly. The fresh air and the water soon relieved them in a great measure.

There had been smoke enough to be seen in the distance; and when the fire was fully extinguished, people began to arrive. The smoke had been seen by some men at work in the field, and they had given the alarm. They were too late to be of any service in putting out the fire; but they took the two children, and conveyed them to the next house.

The older girl was not so badly burned as the boys feared in the beginning. She and the little one had evidently begun to scream before her dress took fire, probably terrified when they saw the flames running up the wooden wall. It takes longer to tell the story than it did for the fire to get under way. The boys were not far from the house when they heard the screams; and the child's clothes could not have been burning more than a moment when they came to her relief.

The girl's hands, and her limbs near the knees, were considerably burned, and she had received injury enough to cause her great pain. The farmer and his two men were the first to arrive; but the fire was out, and the good man gave all his attention to the sufferer. His house was but a short distance from the cottage; and he carried her there, assisted by one of his men. On his arrival he sent his companion for the doctor.

Before he could reach his home, an engine from the town, which was not half a mile distant, rushed to the scene of the fire. The foreman examined the premises, but he could not find any fire. He bustled about for a time while he made his examination, but there was nothing else for him to do.

"It came very near burning the house," said he to Ash Burton, who showed him over the premises, and explained the situation. "How did it take fire?"

"The girl was in so much pain that I did not ask her any questions," replied Ash, as he led the fireman into the front room, in which the family lived. "There is a kerosene-lamp on the floor, and the fire began there. The shade is broken, and perhaps the girl dropped the lamp on the floor after she had lighted it."

"What was she doing with a lamp in the middle of the afternoon?" asked the foreman.

"That is more than I know; but it looks as though the fire was caused by dropping the lamp on the floor," replied Ash.

"It was lucky for the owner that you happened to be near," continued the fireman. "Where were you when you saw the fire?"

"We were just coming around that bend in the road when we heard the screams of the children. We did not see the fire at first. When we got here the doors were all fastened, and we had to beat in the back one with a stick of wood. We put out the fire in the girl's clothes first, and then we poured water on the flames."

As the man asked more questions, Ash explained fully the manner in which they had treated the girl, and then put out the fire.

"You have saved the house; and if you had been a minute later, the little girl might have lost her life. You boys have done remarkably well. You have been brave and resolute, and you have managed the fire with excellent judgment," said the foreman, when he had learned all the facts. "Most boys would have continued to throw water on the fire in the room below; but you went up-stairs, where alone the fire could be checked. You have done well; and the whole fire-department of Genverres, if it had been here, could not have accomplished any more, or done it more neatly."

"Ash Burton was the leader of the party, and he found all the brains," said Chick Penny magnanimously.

"That's so; we followed his lead," added Sam Spottwood; and the others expressed their assent.

"I thank you, sir, for what you have said. I tried to do the best I could, and I am glad we succeeded; for I am sure I could not have done any thing if the other fellows had not worked like firemen. They all behaved first-rate, and did not give up when the smoke had strained their eyes nearly out of their heads," returned Ash, giving his companions the credit they deserved.

"There is nothing for us to do here, and we may as well return to our quarters. I am afraid that child is badly burned, and we will stop at the house where she is," continued the foreman, giving his men the order to return.

The rope of the engine was not very heavily manned, and the six boys were permitted to take part in dragging the machine back to town; and this, to the average boy, is supposed to be fun, however it may be with full-grown men. They were all well rested after the work they had done, and they had even forgotten for the time the unpleasant results of the cruise of the Goldwing. The engine stopped at the next house, where the farmer lived. Ash Burton and the foreman went in to inquire about the sufferer.

"I am keeping her quite comfortable by putting cold water on the burns about once a minute," said the farmer's wife. "I don't know as the doctor will approve of it when he comes, and I should not apply my remedy if the burns were on the head or body. For burns in any other places, cold water is my remedy, because it deadens the pain at once."

"How does the girl seem?" asked the foreman.

"She is pretty badly burned, but she will get over it without any trouble. I always told Mrs. Sankland that she ought not to lock up the children when she went out to work; but the poor woman has a terrible hard time of it, and I suppose she could not help it, for she has to earn enough to get food for her family," replied the good woman.

"But she has a son," suggested the fireman.

"It would be a good deal better for her if she had no son, for he is a good-for-nothing fellow. He won't work to earn any thing, or even take care of the children while his mother is at work. She has to feed him, and it would be a good thing if she had one less mouth to fill."

"He is a bad boy, and runs with Tom Topover, which is enough to condemn any boy," added the fireman.

Ash Burton and his companions winced under this remark, and they were glad they had gone so far as to resolve to avoid him in the future.

"My husband would give the boy work all summer, and pay him all he could earn; but he will not do a thing, and he is worrying the life out of his mother," continued the farmer's wife. "I think something ought to be done with him; and it would be a good thing if he could be sent to the house of correction, or some other institution, where he could be made to work."

The foreman of the engine quite agreed with her, and promised to inquire into the matter on his return to the town. The march, for it was not a run on the return, was resumed with the machine, which soon reached its destination. Several persons who kept horses had ridden out to see where the fire was, and the report of what had happened was already in circulation through the place.

It was not more than four o'clock, and the reformed Topovers — as they regarded themselves — were not inclined to go home until they had done something about the cruise of the Goldwing. As they came out of the engine-house, they saw Captain Gildrock in his buggy. He had stopped in the street, and was talking to a fireman who had just left the engine.

The reformers halted, and decided to hail the principal as soon as he finished his conversation with the man. The latter seemed to be talking to him very earnestly, and pointed down the street. Suddenly the captain turned his horse in the direction the man had pointed, and drove off so rapidly that the boys could not hail him. He turned the next corner, and the boys followed him.

They had gone to another corner when they saw the captain's team standing at the door of a mechanic's shop. He had left the vehicle, and secured the horse by a weight. Sam suggested that he was getting out a warrant for the arrest of those who had stolen the sloop; but Ash was confident that no magistrate lived on that street, which was occupied mainly by mechanics' shops and small factories.

"I don't want to miss him next time," said Ash. "I should like to have this business settled, or at least to know what is going to be done about it, before I go home. Captain Gildrock goes off like a rifle-shot when he starts, and seems to be thinking of something all the time."

"That's so," Sam replied. "We don't want to disturb him while he is busy about something. I will go around to the main street, and stop him if he comes out that way."

This suggestion was approved and adopted. Sam and two of the party went around, and soon appeared at the other end of the street, for they did not want to be seen till the principal had time to attend to them.

It was all of half an hour before Captain Gildrock appeared.

CHAPTER X.

TWO CONFLICTING STORIES.

CAPTAIN GILDROCK turned his horse, and started on his return by the way he had come. As Ash Burton and the others saw, he was engaged in deep thought, and had his eyes fixed on the floor of the buggy. He seemed to be engaged in some important business; but Ash decided, at once, that the circumstances were enough to warrant him in disturbing his reflections.

"Captain Gildrock!" called the leader of the party, stepping into the street where he was about to pass.

The principal reined in his horse, and seemed to come out of the reverie in which he had been buried.

"We should like to speak to you, sir, when you are ready to hear us," continued Ash.

"I am ready to hear you now, if you have a

short story to tell; but I am in a hurry," replied the captain, rather briskly.

"Then we will wait till you have more time, sir; we will call at your house when you are not busy," added Ash, who did not think it wise to ask the principal to sit in judgment upon their case when he was in a flurry of excitement.

"Very well; come to my house this evening at any time after half-past six," said the captain, as he started his horse. But he suddenly reined him in, and took a piece of paper from his pocket. "Do you know a young man by the name of Ashley Burton, and another by the name of Samuel Spottwood?" he asked.

"My name is Ashley Burton, sir; and I wanted to see you about the wrong we have done in taking the boat on Beechwater," replied Ash, rather sheepishly.

"About the wrong you did!" exclaimed the principal, opening his eyes as though a new revelation had just been made to him.

"Yes, sir; and I have six dollars in my pocket, the earnings of the Goldwing, which belongs to you, or to Dory Dornwood," continued Ash, carrying out the good resolution of himself and his penitent companions.

"I have been looking for you and the others who were with you," replied the captain, biting his lip as though things had not happened just as he expected.

"We are all here, sir," answered Ash, as he looked up the street, and saw Sam and his party running towards them. "We are very sorry for what we have done, and we will promise never again to touch one of your boats without permission."

"But I hear very bad stories about you. You were going to take the boat, and, with the money you had earned with her, were going to Burlington to 'have a time,' as Tom Topover called it."

Ash looked at his companion, and there was something like a smile on his face. As he might have supposed, Tom had told his own story, and cast all the blame upon the members of the party he had left at the point.

"Not a word has been said in my hearing about going to Burlington, or any other place," replied Ash; and his companions said the same thing.

"I have been led to believe that Ashley Burton and Samuel Spottwood were the ringleaders of the enterprise, and that Topover, Digfield, Sankland,

and the others we found on board of the Goldwing, had been cheated into going into the boat by
you. Then, when they found you meant to leave
them at the point, and go to Burlington, they had
taken possession of the sloop, and were going to
return her to her moorings," said the captain,
smiling while he repeated the substance of Tom
Topover's explanation.

"I suppose you can believe either story you
please, sir. I am willing to tell the truth; and we
all confess that we were very much to blame,
though there was some excuse for our going on
board of the Goldwing in the first place; and I am
sure we did not go to her with the intention of
sailing in her," answered Ash, frankly and openly.

Captain Gildrock seemed to be moved by the
narrative of the speaker. He glanced from one
to another of the penitents till he had examined
all their faces. He did not say that he was impressed in their favor; but their bearing certainly
compared very favorably with that of the original
gang, who were in the majority in the party captured by the Sylph.

"I have been so much annoyed by these attempts to steal the boats of the institution, that I

have decided to put a stop to them," continued the principal, after he had looked over the Burton party. "I intended to prosecute all the offenders engaged in stealing the Goldwing, if I found I could make out a good case; and I am now investigating the matter."

"I hope you will not prosecute us, sir," interposed Ash, very humbly, "for my father cannot very well afford to pay my fine."

"While I was inquiring about you, I heard about the fire which burned the house in which the mother of one of the boys I have on board the Sylph lived; and I was told at first that a little girl, this boy's sister, had been burned to death."

"Not so bad as that, sir," replied Ash.

"I have just been to see the foreman of the engine that went to the fire, and I have obtained all the facts from him," continued Captain Gildrock. "But I can't investigate the case here. If you can come on board of the Sylph, where the six boys I found in the Goldwing are, I think we can soon settle the matter so that I shall know what to do."

"We will go there at once, sir," replied Ash; and all the others assented. "But here is the six dollars paid me for taking out the parties at the picnic."

"No matter about that now," added the principal, as he drove off.

"He did not say a word about what we did at the fire," said Hop Cabright.

"He has just been to see the foreman of the engine, too," said Syl Peckman.

"I don't know that it had any thing to do with the Goldwing or the Topovers," said Sam Spottwood.

"Perhaps not, but we did a good piece of work; and, if we had not come along just as we did, the little girl would have been burned to death, and the house destroyed," argued Hop, who seemed to think that the two events of the day had some connection.

"Do you expect that putting out the fire at the Widow Sankland's will atone for the wrong we did in taking the Goldwing for a sail?" asked Ash, turning to Hop.

"Well, I think it will prove that we are not the worst fellows in the world," replied Hop.

"Do you think if a fireman should kill a man, it would save him from punishment because he had saved a woman from being burned to death?"

"I don't know that I think that, but I think he ought to have the credit of his good deed," answered Hop, stoutly.

"I don't believe it would save his neck from being stretched," persisted Ash, who was assuredly a very good fellow — when he was not led away by some temptation like the desire to sail a boat. "I don't believe that it will make a particle of difference to Captain Gildrock that we put out that fire, and saved the little girl. He is not a milk-and-water man."

This conversation was continued till they reached the grounds of the Industrial School. The boys had been assured of the intention of the principal to prosecute if he could make out a good case. It appeared that Tom Topover had invented some story which failed to explain the manner in which they had first gone on board of the sloop.

They found the entire party which had been away in the yacht still on her deck. The ladies looked with interest upon the additional culprits, as they walked forward where the principal held court.   Lily Bristol was talking to Dory; and they were generally together on board, which caused her to spend the greater portion of her time in the pilot-house. She seemed to have a good deal of pity in her looks as she gazed at them.

Paul Bristol received them when they came on board, as he had been instructed to do, and conducted them to the forecastle, where they found their six companions in the cruise of the Goldwing, under the charge of the relentless quartermaster, who figured so largely in the extreme discipline of the institution. Captain Gildrock had just returned from his visit to the town, and had seated himself near the gangway.

He received the party from the point more kindly than they had expected, and immediately proceeded with the examination of the case. He called out Tom Topover, and said he wished him to repeat the explanation he had made before, in the presence of those whom he charged with being the ringleaders in the adventure. Tom grinned as though he was as innocent as a lamb on the hills, and went into his narrative without any hesitation.

According to Tom's version, Ash Burton and

the other five who had just come on board had taken the boat, and were going out upon the lake in her. He and the rest of the party captured had been in the grove, when Ash brought the boat up to the wharf, and said they had permission from the principal to use her, and finally persuaded them to join the excursion.

"Persuaded you, did they? If they had permission to use the boat, how did it happen that you needed any persuasion?" asked the captain.

"We did not believe they got leave to take the boat. They coaxed us to go with them, and were willing to take their oath that it was straight about the boat. We gave in then," replied Tom. "When we got to the point, and found a picnic there, Ash Burton went ashore, and offered to let the boat for two dollars an hour. The folks there took him up, and he carried out three loads, and got six dollars for it."

"Then it was Ashley Burton who first proposed to take out the parties?"

"Of course it was. He made all of us go on shore, and stay there three hours. Then we overheard one of them telling another, that they would leave us at the point, and go to Burlington, and spend the money. But I got ahead of them," chuckled Tom. "When Ash Burton went to dinner, I got my fellows into the boat, and we started for home, to carry the boat back to you. That's the whole of it."

"I am glad it is," replied the captain, turning to the six from the shore. "Now we will hear the other side of the story."

Ash Burton related it, and the others were called upon to indorse the statement if it was the truth; and they did so without any qualification. Their leader had related the simple truth, and had not put in any excuses for himself or his friends.

"That's all a lie!" exclaimed Tom, looking as though he was shocked to hear so many falsehoods crowded into a short story.

"You say it was Ashley that first proposed to take out the parties, Topover?" added the principal.

Tom persisted that it was, and the others backed him. Captain Gildrock called Paul Bristol, and by him sent an order to Dory to get the yacht under way again. In a few minutes she was standing down Beechwater to the outlet.

CHAPTER XI.

COMPLIMENTARY TO THE PICNIC-PARTY.

THE penitents had never been on board of the Sylph before; and, even in the midst of the examination which was to decide what was to be done with them for the misdemeanor of the forenoon, they enjoyed the motion of the yacht. Tom and his companions were prisoners on the forecastle; and, though nothing had been said to the penitents, they considered themselves in the same condition. They had heard of Bates, who was the ogre of the institution to bad boys; and there he was, acting as a deck-hand.

Paul Bristol attended to the stern-line, against which the steamer backed to throw her head out from the wharf. Sometimes he had served as fireman; but a man was now employed for that service, and the engineer's son was a man-of-all-work. He had learned something about the engine, so that he could attend to it for a short time; and Dory had instructed him in piloting, so that he could take the wheel when it was plain sailing.

Lily Bristol went to the pilot-house with the captain when he was ordered to get under way. She wondered where they were going, but she had taken little interest in the examination on the forecastle. Captain Dornwood told her, with a pleasant smile, that it was not customary for officers and seamen to ask questions in regard to the movements of the vessel: all they had to do was to obey the orders of their superior officers. A soldier or a sailor who asked questions before he did what he was directed to do, was good for nothing.

"But you are the captain of the steamer, Dory," said she, as the young gentleman politely ushered her into the pilot-house.

" When we have the ship's company on board, I am the captain; though even then it is only a position in name, for I have to obey the orders of the owner," replied Dory. "But, now that we are not in commission, not much attention is paid to rank; and sometimes when my uncle is at the wheel I act as deck-hand."

"What do you mean by being in commission, Dory? Have you any commission?" asked Lily.

"That's what my uncle calls it when we have the regular ship's company on board. A ship in the navy, or a yacht, is said to be in commission when she has her officers and men on board, and is in condition for going to sea, or doing what is required of her."

"You don't go to sea; but you go to lake, just the same now as when you have thirty or forty on duty," laughed Lily.

"But Captain Gildrock don't call us in commission when we use the steamer with our present crew: that's all the difference there is. Three persons can handle the Sylph very well; and four is enough to work her comfortably, though not when there are any meals to be served."

Just then, as the steamer was standing across the little lake towards the outlet, Paul Bristol appeared at the door of the pilot-house, with the order of the principal to run to the point where the picnic was, and make a landing at the wharf.

"To the point where the picnic is, and make a landing at the wharf," repeated Captain Dornwood; and Paul touched his hat and retired, possibly thinking that his company was not wanted there.

"Didn't you hear him? What makes you say it over after him?" asked Lily, as her brother was leaving.

"My uncle requires us to repeat all orders, so as to be sure that they are understood, as they do in the navy, where he served several years when he was a young man. We do every thing in navy fashion when we are in commission, and we keep up some of the forms even now," replied the captain.

"What are we going to the picnic for, I wonder," added Lily.

"I haven't the least idea. I have learned to conquer my curiosity, or at least not to let it get the better of me," laughed Dory.

"But Captain Gildrock has all the boys now that were out in the Goldwing. What do you suppose he is going to do with them?"

"I haven't the least idea. I should as soon think of asking the minister what he is going to preach about next Sunday, as of asking my uncle what he is going to do."

"I should think he would tell you without asking."

"Sometimes he does, but not often; and when we are going to do any thing on shore, or on board of the boats, the orders come as a surprise to us."

As the steamer approached the mouth of the river, Captain Gildrock came on the hurricane deck, but he did not even look into the pilot-house. He began to walk up and down, and Lily watched him for a few minutes with interest.

"He looks as though he had something in his head now," said Dory, as he observed the thoughtful expression of his uncle.

"He must be thinking about those boys," suggested Lily.

"Very likely: they have been a great nuisance to us, for they have stolen the boats a great many times before (that is, the row-boats), when they have been left on shore."

"Do you know those boys?"

"Some of them: we have had some dealings with the Topovers when they ran away with the barges. But there is a lot of new fellows among them now that I hardly know by sight. Within a week I have heard my uncle drop some few remarks about the bad boys of Genverres, as though he was thinking about them. This affair with the Goldwing is perhaps the text of his thoughts. But it will all come out, if there is any thing, very soon."

The Sylph stood across the mouth of the bay, and made her landing at the rude wharf (and it was so rude, that Dory had to be very careful in handling the yacht, or she would have stove it all to pieces). When it was evident that she was going to stop there, the picknickers hurried to the wharf to see her, for she was a great curiosity to people who did not live near the lake. The present party were from twelve miles inland, and intended to drive back to their home by moonlight.

"Can we be permitted to go on board, and look at this steamer?" asked the gentleman who had employed Ash Burton to sail the party in the forenoon, as he hailed Captain Gildrock on the hurricane deck. "Our people have never seen such a steamer as this appears to be, and their curiosity is excited."

"How many people have you?" asked the principal.

"About eighty-five."

"We have room enough for the whole of them,

then ; and I shall be happy to have them take a
little trip in her," added the captain.

"You are very kind, sir ; and your invitation is
very unexpected. We are very glad to accept,
especially as we do not start for home till eight
o'clock," replied Mr. Murdock, the manager of
the party.

"I have a little business with you, sir; and,
after your party are on board, I should like to see
you in the pilot-house."

"Business with me ? " exclaimed Mr. Murdock,
greatly surprised.

"In regard to the boys who took some of your
party out to sail," Captain Gildrock explained.

The picnickers were delighted with the invita-
tation, and accepted it with enthusiasm. They
crowded on board so eagerly, that the principal
interfered to prevent them from breaking the
wharf down with their weight. They were soon
on board, and the order was given to Captain
Dornwood to back out from the pier.

The picnic-party had a band of music with
them, and they enlivened the occasion with their
music. The passengers satisfied their curiosity
first, and the principal conducted Mr. Murdock

all over the vessel. The examination ended at the pilot-house, which both of them entered. To the inquiries made by Captain Gildrock, the gentleman gave him all the information he required. He had hailed the Goldwing as she was passing the point; and the young man who was steering the boat objected, at first, to taking any passengers.

As the captain suspected, Tom's story was a tissue of lies, and that of Ash Burton and his companions seemed to be the simple truth. The principal explained that the sloop was used without permission of the owner, upon which Mr. Murdock assured him that he would not have employed her if he had known the fact.

"The fellow they called Tom Topover is an unmitigated young scoundrel," he added; "while the one who sailed our parties behaved like a gentleman, and seemed to understand his business very well."

"I think I comprehend the case very well now, but I am very much embarrassed about it," added Captain Gildrock, whose brow was contracted with the thought that he was giving to the subject. "If Tom Topover and his gang, who have robbed my fruit-trees till I built fences so high that they could not get over them, were all of the culprits, I should prosecute them at once, though it would only compel their parents, who are poor people, to pay their fines. Ashley Burton and the rest of the boys who were left on shore at the picnic are better boys; and I cannot think of taking them to the court, now that I have got at the facts."

"It is a difficult matter to manage," added Mr. Murdock.

"I cannot prosecute half the culprits, and ·let the other half escape; for they are all equally guilty of the offence against the law. But Burton and his companions came to me, very penitent, with the money the boat had earned; while Tom and his companions lied till they were black in the face. As you say, it is a difficult case to manage. I shall have to find some other remedy for my grievances besides a court of justice."

The principal had learned all the facts he wished to know. Tom had lied to him; while Ash and his party had voluntarily told the whole truth, and manifested a genuine penitence. He was sure the latter would give him no further trouble. The business settled, Captain Gildrock devoted himself to the party on board, and made them as happy as he could. He pointed out all the objects of interest on the lake, including Split Rock, which finds a place in the guide-books. When he landed them at the wharf, they were profuse in their expressions of gratitude for the pleasant trip he had given them.

At the wharf, Tom Topover and his companions attempted to escape by getting into the crowd of picnickers as they were going on shore; but Bates had been directed to take charge of them, and he had his eyes on them. Tom found himself taken by the collar, and hurled to the deck. The others retreated to the bow, where they had been ordered to remain. Tom Topover was as mad as a March hare when he rose to his feet. He began to indulge in some foul talk, when Bates collared him again and pitched him into the bow. He showed some signs of resistance.

"Shut up!" said Bates, in a low tone.

Tom looked at him. The old quartermaster was not the kind of person he liked to deal with, and he concluded to obey him. In fact, the bully did most of his fighting with his tongue, and generally found a way to back out when it came to hard blows.

The party on shore gave three cheers for the steamer and her polite owner, the band played a parting strain, and the steamer whistled a return of the compliments paid to her as she departed for her wharf.

Captain Gildrock was still in deep thought. In fact, he had done a great deal of heavy thinking over the very problem which now occupied his mind, during the entire summer. But he said nothing to any one, and Lily and Captain Dornwood chatted as merrily as ever in the pilot-house. When he landed, the principal went to his library, attended by Ash and his penitent companions.

CHAPTER XII.

A NEW MISSION FOR THE BEECH-HILL SCHOOL.

IT was within two weeks of the time for the opening of the Beech-Hill Industrial School. Only one-half of the students for the coming year had been engaged, and this was the circumstance which had given the principal so much thought during the summer. It was not that there was a lack of applicants; for, while he could accept only sixteen in addition to the number which remained over, he had more than a hundred applications for admission.

The subject had almost elevated itself to a question of political economy in the mind of the old shipmaster. He found that more than one-half of his pupils in the past had been the sons of wealthy or well-to-do people, who were abundantly able to pay for the tuition of their sons, iucluding all the branches pursued in his school.

He had come to the conclusion that he could make a better use of his money than in educating the children of those who were able to pay for it. The institution was no longer an experiment, and the most important question was in regard to those who should be selected to receive its benefits.

Captain Gildrock had come to feel that he ought to provide for those who were not able to provide for themselves. He could render a greater service to the community in which he lived, by fitting for usefulness those who were neglected by their parents, or who could not be controlled by them, than by instructing those who needed no assistance. He had demonstrated the problem he had undertaken to solve, and now he felt that he ought to make the school as serviceable as possible to the State.

With this question in his mind he had looked over the list of applicants, with the description of each. Against nearly the whole of the questions in the printed form of application, which related to the financial ability of the parents, it was written that they were wealthy, or that they were well off. With his new views of duty, he had been able to select only four whom he was willing to accept. He would not take pupils at a price, and those who were able to pay for the education they desired for their sons could establish such a school as that at Beech Hill.

The taking of the Goldwing, and the capture of Tom Topover and his gang, intensified his reflections over the problem. If he could reform and reconstruct such bruisers, and make them capable of taking care of themselves, as well as become useful members of society, he would render a more acceptable service to the community than he could by instructing boys whose parents were able to pay their tuition-bills.

The event narrated in this story enabled him to come to a conclusion. He knew all about the Topovers. They had been a nuisance in the town for years, and their parents could do nothing with them. They would not work, though their parents needed the little they could earn. They were very irregular at school when they pretended to go, and they had no correct views in regard to the rights of property. So far as he could inform himself, they had average ability, and were capable of being made into decent men, to say the least.

Of the original Topovers there were only four, though they had been recruited by two more as rough as themselves. These were the six who had been captured in the Goldwing; and they were now on the forecastle, in charge of Bates, while the six who had put out the fire were with the captain in his library. The principal had considered what effect the admission to the school of such fellows as Tom Topover, Kidd Digfield, and the others would have upon the *morale* and the discipline of the institution. If he could not reform them, he could keep them under a sharp discipline, and they would have little power to contaminate others.

" Ashley Burton, I have finished my examination of this case ; and I shall not prosecute you, as I intended at first," said the principal, opening the subject of the interview.

" Thank you, sir ! " exclaimed Sam Spottwood.

The others said as much as this, and they were certainly very grateful to the captain for his indulgence.

" I took out the picnic-party for the purpose of ascertaining the facts. The gentleman in charge of the party spoke very well of you, and fully confirmed the statement you made to me. I think you are sincerely penitent for the wrong you have done. If you had left the Goldwing at the wharf when you went ashore first, I should have found no fault with you for taking her, I should say that you had done just right; though it was constructively and technically wrong for you to unmoor the boat, even if you had lost your dinner and your supper. I am not a close constructionist."

"You are very kind, sir," added Sam, who was more demonstrative than the others.

"I had started in my buggy to intercept you as you came home from the picnic. On my way, there was an alarm of fire; and I soon heard that the house of the Widow Sankland had been burned, and one of the children had lost its life. This was a mistake, for I met the engine returning from the fire. I went to see Captain Linder, who is the foreman of the company; and he spoke in the highest terms of your conduct, and the good judgment you used in managing the fire. No doubt you saved the life of the child, and the house from total destruction."

"Ash Burton was the leader, and told us what to do," interposed Sam Spottwood.

"You all did well, and you are worthy of praise. What you did at the fire is not an offset for the wrong you did on the lake; for a good deed will not balance an evil one, though it may modify our judgment of the evil-doer. I have nothing more to say to you now, and I am confident you will not again meddle with any property of the institution."

"We will not, sir," replied Ash, as he took the dozen half-dollars from his pocket, and tendered them to the principal. "These do not belong to me, or to any of us. They were earned with Dory's boat."

"The money certainly does not belong to you; and, obtained as it was, I am not willing that you should retain and enjoy it," replied the principal. "We do not let the boats under any circumstances, and we do not need any money they might earn. I have spoken to Dory about the matter, and he left it entirely to me. I have decided what shall be done with it. It shall be given to the Widow Sankland, who needs it more than you or your parents, though they may not be very well off. You may carry the money to her to-night, Ashley, if you are willing to do so."

" Perfectly willing, sir; and I will go as soon as I have had my supper," replied Ash; and the party left the house with lighter hearts than they had entered it, for the terrible fear of prosecution no longer confronted them.

Captain Gildrock did not say a word in regard to the other culprits in taking the sloop, and the Burton party wondered if the principal intended to bring them up before the court. Hop Cabright was sure that he would not do so, for he would have served them all alike. Syl Peckman was confident that he did not mean to let them off as he had their party, for they had been captured on board of the sloop. Ash and Sam had no opinion, and said it was impossible to say what such a man as Captain Gildrock would do, for he was different from all the other men in Genverres.

They went to their suppers; and all the questions asked them by their parents related to the fire, and the child they had saved. Nothing was said about the Goldwing, and probably nothing was known about the scrape from which they had so happily escaped.

They met after supper, and walked over to the house they had saved from destruction. They found the Widow Sankland there with her two children. The one who had been burned was on the bed ; but she was quite comfortable, for the doctor had prescribed the continuance of the cold water, which was renewed every few minutes. The farmer and his wife had been there, and done what they could to make the house habitable after the fire and water had done so much mischief.

The widow received the money which Ash presented to her, with many thanks. She had no money, for she had not received the pay for her day's work. She said she was very poor indeed, and it was only with the hardest struggle that she earned enough to feed her children, to say nothing of clothing them.

Mrs. Sankland explained that her daughter had lighted the lamp to go down cellar for some milk for the little one. She had dropped it on the floor, and the fluid had taken fire, from which her dress had caught when she tried to put it out.

" Have you seen any thing of Pelham to-day ? " asked the widow. " He must have heard of the fire, and he ought to have come home. He could help a good deal if he only would. He could take care of the children while I am at work, but he won't even do that."

Sam Spottwood told her that Pell had been captured with the other Topovers; and Ash added the rest of the story, that they had been in the scrape.

"Something must be done with him, for I cannot do any thing with him. He won't mind me any more than if I wasn't his mother," said the widow, wiping the tears from her thin face.

"He will be at home soon, I should think," added Ash.

"It does not make much difference whether he comes or not: he does me no good, and I have to feed him. I wish something might be done with him, for he is a bad boy."

The boys departed much impressed by the confessions of the poor woman; and they wished they were rich, like Captain Gildrock, that they might help her. But Ash Burton was willing to go a point beyond wishing that he was rich, and he decided to apply to some of the wealthy people of the town for assistance in clothing and food for her. But the boys had not gone ten rods from the house before they met the carriage of the rich man of the Beech-Hill estate. Dory and his mother were with the captain; and, as he stopped his horses in front of the cottage, Dory took a large basket from the carriage. He carried it into the house, and then returned to take care of the horses while his uncle· and his mother went in. They never heard of a case of distress within ten miles of their home without doing all they could to relieve it.

Mr. Sankland had been a laborer who worked on the farms in the vicinity. He was not a thrifty man, and he drank too much whiskey for his reliability. He had died less than a year before, leaving nothing at all; though his wife had saved enough from her own earnings to bury him. When she could get work, she did tolerably well, especially washing that she could take home with her. In summer there were people boarding in the town, and at the farmhouses in the vicinity, who gave her their work; but in winter it had been almost a starving time with her. In the spring an agency for a laundry had been established in the place, and Mrs. Sankland lost most of her customers.

Mrs. Dornwood presented her with the contents

of the basket, which consisted mainly of meats and vegetables brought from the provision store, and groceries from another establishment. The poor woman was glad to get these things, and she soon told the history of her miseries. She repeated what she had said to the young firemen about her son, and it ended in the captain's asking her if she was willing to put the boy in his care. She was willing and glad to do so.

CHAPTER XIII.

THE BEGINNING OF THE TROUBLE.

CAPTAIN GILDROCK drew from his pocket a paper he had drawn up for the widow to sign. He read it to her, explaining its meaning as he proceeded. It was a contract by which, in consideration of her son's board, clothing, and tuition, she surrendered to the principal the entire charge of the boy for three years. Mrs. Sankland was entirely satisfied with the document, and signed it without any hesitation.

"He shall be as well treated as the rest of the boys in the institution, but he must obey orders; and he will have no time to roam about the streets and fields," said the principal. "It is necessary that he should be subjected to strict discipline; and no violence will be used unless he shows fight, or refuses to obey an order."

"He needs a good whipping more than any thing else," added his mother, as she wiped the tears from her eyes. "He has done nothing for me; and I cannot afford to support a great fellow like him in idleness, when he will not even take care of the children while I am at my work."

"I shall try to make a man of him, Mrs. Sankland; and, if no one interferes with me, I think I shall succeed," added Captain Gildrock, as he moved towards the door.

"There is no one on earth to interfere with you, sir, except me; and I am too glad to have him taken care of to meddle with any one who is so kind as to take care of him," replied the poor widow.

The principal and his sister returned to the carriage, and the captain drove to the house of Tom Topover's father. He was a laboring man, who worked very hard to support a large family; and Tom was the oldest of the children. But they lived in comfort and plenty compared with the Widow Sankland. Neither the father nor the mother was a person of much force, though they got along very well in the world.

"I called to see you, Mr. Topover, in regard to your son Thomas," the captain began, when the introduction had been disposed of.

"He is a bad boy, Captain Gildrock; and I know that he has given you a deal of trouble at one time and another," said the father, who felt that he was very unfortunate in having such a son; though he closed his eyes to the fact that he had spoiled the boy by indulgence years before.

"I am afraid you are not far from right, Mr. Topover," replied the captain.

"What has he been doing now, sir? I am sorry he was not sent to the house of correction when he was taken up on the other side of the lake. Has he been troubling you again?" asked the man.

The principal explained what Tom had been doing, relating the events of the day in connection with the Goldwing.

"I am sorry for it, sir; but I can't do any thing with the boy. I have talked with him, and I have thrashed him till I am tired of it. What can I do with him?" asked the poor father, puzzled by the situation.

"I intended to prosecute the boys the next time they stole any of the boats," continued the principal.

"Do it, sir. I shall not object to any thing

you do with my boy, for he deserves the worst he is likely to get for his bad behavior," replied the father.

"He will be condemned to a fine, and you will have to pay it," suggested Captain Gildrock.

"I will not pay it! I have done that twice, and I shall not do it again," protested Mr. Topover.

"Then he will stand committed till the fine is paid."

"So much the better!" exclaimed the desperate parent. "I have no money to waste on a boy who treats me as Tom does. He won't do a thing about the house; and, when he is out late, he makes his mother get his supper for him when he comes in. He is a bad boy, sir; and, if they keep him in jail for six months, I will not say a word."

"He needs a little sharp discipline."

"That he does! He hasn't been near the house since morning, and we may not see him to-night till nine or ten o'clock. Then he will want his supper, and a piece of bread and butter and some pie will not be enough for him. He makes such a row, that his mother has to cook something for him, even if the fires are all out."

"He seems to be a perfect tyrant in the house," added the principal with a smile, as he realized that the boy had been spoiled by his parents.

"That's just what he is. If he don't get what he wants, he makes such a row that he wakes all the children, and we have trouble half the night."

"He will not come home to-night, unless you wish to have him do so," said Captain Gildrock, coming nearer to his point.

"I don't care if he never comes into the house again," protested Mr. Topover.

"You don't mean that, Richard,' mildly interposed his wife. "I wish the boy could be taken care of, but I don't want him to come to any harm."

The principal took a paper like that he had read at the Widow Sankland's, adapted to the case of Tom Topover. He read it, after he had proposed that the vagrant boy should be admitted to the Beech-Hill Industrial School. He explained its meaning fully.

"We shall make him obey orders, but we shall

use him as well as he will allow us to do," continued Captain Glanrock. "If both of you will sign this paper, I will keep him at the institution until the term begins. He will be fed, clothed, and instructed, and obliged to work at some trade. I think we should make a mechanic of him, for he seems to have a taste for working with tools upon iron."

"But Tom won't agree to it," replied Mr. Tapper.

"I haven't asked him to agree to it, and I don't intend to do any thing of the sort. You are his father, and his legal guardian; you can do any thing you please with him, so long as you don't abuse him," continued Captain Glanrock sharply; for he did not like the disposition to temporize with a serious case.

"I should be very glad to have him go to your school, Captain Glanrock," added the father.

"So should I, and I should be easy about him all the time if he were only there," said Mrs. Tapper.

"Then all you have to do is to sign this paper. His father's name would be enough to answer the law, but I prefer to have his mother's also."

"When he comes home he will make a terrible row, and"—

"He won't come home till he is in a frame of mind to be decent and respectful to both of you," interposed the captain.

"I will sign the paper," said Mr. Tepevee, after some hesitation. "I can't do any thing with him; and, to tell the truth, Captain Gildrock, I don't believe you can."

"Perhaps I can't: I don't know. I am willing to try; and I believe the boy can be saved, though he will need sharp discipline."

Both the father and the mother seemed to be afraid of the tyrant son, and this was the trouble with them. But they signed the paper after a good deal of delay; though the principal did not urge them to do so, and took no means to conceal the fact that the boy would be subjected to severe discipline.

The captain left the house, promising to report to the parents upon the progress of the son. In the same manner he visited the homes of Kidd Digfield and Nim Splugger. The father of the former was a blacksmith; and he had done his best to get his son into his shop to blow and strike for him, but he had utterly failed. The boy would promise any thing, but he did not keep his promises. He was much pleased with the idea of having his son admitted to the school, and signed the paper presented to him, as did his wife, without any objection or hesitation.

The father of Nimrod Splugger was a German shoemaker, who had married a Vermont woman. Both the father and mother seemed to be totally indifferent in regard to the welfare of the boy, and they were willing to sign any thing that relieved them from the burden of feeding and clothing him. The principal's business at the home of the German was soon finished; and he drove back to the mansion, leaving two more cases to be disposed of in the morning.

The six captured young rascals had been left on board of the Sylph, in charge of Mr. Bristol and Bates. After the party on board had taken supper in the forward cabin, the young ruffians were marched in, and they had satisfied their appetites with the good things set before them; and their imprisonment did not seem to impair their ability to eat and drink.

After the meal they had been taken back to

the forecastle. Tom and the bolder of the vagrants growled, and threatened evil things to those who detained them; but they made no attempt to escape, for they saw that it would be useless. When the captain appeared, at about nine o'clock in the evening, he called out Raglan Spinner and Benjamin Sinker, whose parents he had not been able to see for the want of time, and dismissed them. They were not quite as enterprising as Tom and Kidd; but they were not a whit better, and no more disposed to obey their parents.

Captain Gildrock made no explanations to the two he discharged, and the young ruffians concluded that they had fully atoned for their offence by the imprisonment they had suffered. They were to take a different view of the matter the next day.

The principal went to the forecastle, where the four ruffians were to be seen under the awning, by the light of a lantern which hung over their heads. Neither of their custodians had said any thing to them, and did not encourage any talk on their part. They asked questions about what was to be done with them;

but Bates did not know, and would not have answered if he had known. When they saw the captain, they had worked themselves up to the height of discontent. They were accustomed to have their own way; and any restraint was a burden to them, even if it subjected them to no discomfort.

"I want to go home," growled Tom Topover as soon as he saw the principal. "I'm not going to stay here all night."

"You will not stay here all night," answered Captain Gildrock, in his mild tones. "Bates, you will take them to the dormitory, and give them four rooms at the farther end on the left."

"On the left, sir; I understand," replied the old quartermaster.

On the outside of the windows of these rooms was an iron grating like that used in banks to cover the operations of the cashier or teller. They had been fitted up for those who were disposed to run away. Besides the locks on the doors, there were crossbars across each of them, secured by padlocks, so that they could not be removed.

"Mr. Bristol and I will assist you," added

the captain, when he saw that four of the young ruffians might be more than a handful for the old man, though he was still strong and active.

"I want to go home," growled Tom again, when he found that no notice had been taken of his complaint.

"You will not go home, and you will come with me," continued the principal.

The trouble began then.

CHAPTER XIV.

THE PRISONERS IN THE DORMITORY.

CAPTAIN GILDROCK had already directed Dory and Paul to prepare the four rooms indicated for the reception of the new pupils. They were furnished with good beds, and were far more luxurious than the rooms the ruffians occupied at home.

"I'm not going with you!" yelled Tom angrily. "I am going home, and you haven't any right to keep me here!"

Captain Gildrock did not wait to hear any more. He took Tom by the collar with his right hand, while he grasped Nim Splugger with the other. Tom lay down upon the deck, and refused to move; but this made no difference to the stalwart principal, who dragged him along as though he had been nothing but a small parcel.

Nim Splugger always followed his leader, and he lay down also; but both of them were dragged to the forward gangway, where the principal dropped them. Dory and Paul, having put the rooms in order, had come to the wharf. But the captain would not employ any pupil to assist in managing another. Tom lay upon the deck, too obstinate to get up; and Nim pursued the same policy.

The principal took a rope, and tied the hands of Tom behind him, and then made him fast to a stanchion. Taking Nim by the collar, he led or dragged him to the dormitory, where he locked him into his room. The engineer and the deck-hand did as much for Pell Sankland and Kidd Digfield. Each was crowded into a room by himself, and left to his own reflections.

They returned to the steamer to dispose of Tom. In spite of his struggles, he was taken to his room. He fought, kicked, and tried to lie down; but, in the hands of two men, he was utterly powerless. As soon as he was in the apartment assigned to him, the principal removed the cord that bound his hands behind him.

" This will be your room for the future," said Captain Gildrock, without a particle of anger or indignation in his tones or his looks.

"I'm not going to stay here! I want to go home!" protested Tom, so mad that he could not help crying like a great baby.

"This is your home, and you will stay here," added the principal gently.

"I tell you I won't stay here! I don't belong to your school, and you have no right to keep me here!" howled the chief ruffian.

"Perhaps I have. I advise you to cool off, and take things calmly," continued the captain, as he took the papers which had been signed that evening from his pocket. "I might prosecute you, and you would be condemned to pay a heavy fine."

"My father would pay it: I would make him pay it."

"On the contrary, he will pay no more fines on your account."

"Yes, he will!"

"More than that, he will not be called upon to pay any," replied Captain Gildrock, selecting the agreement with Mr. Topover from the bundle. "You are now a member of the Beech-Hill Industrial School, and you will be as well used as your conduct will allow; but you will learn to obey orders."

"I am not a member of the school, and I would not be!" replied Tom. "I never joined, and I shall not join!"

"Perhaps you would like to read this paper," added the captain, handing it to him.

The ruffian was scholar enough to make out the meaning of the document at once. He had cooled off to some extent, and the contents of the paper seemed to be a great surprise to him. He read it a second time, before he raised his eyes from the writing.

"Did my father and mother sign that paper?" asked he, as the principal took the document from his hand before he had thought of tearing it up.

"You can see for yourself that they did," replied Captain Gildrock. "You won't obey them, and you are of no use to them, and have made them no end of trouble."

"I don't believe they signed it. They had no right to sign it without saying any thing to me," blustered Tom.

"I think they had a perfect right to do so, and they have done it. The paper gives me entire control of you for the next three years, and you have no power to escape it."

"But I won't stay here!"

"I will see to that part of the agreement," added the captain, with a smile.

"My father and mother will catch fits the next time I see them," moaned Tom, beginning to realize the situation.

"I shall take care that you don't see them until you are in a proper frame of mind to do so."

"They have put me into this school for three years without saying a word to me!" blubbered Tom, rising from his chair, and beginning to walk about the room.

"It was not necessary to consult you. Your parents have the right to dispose of you as they think best, as long as they do not subject you to any abuse. They have placed you at this school; and you may depend upon it, that you will stay here, and that you will obey orders. If you behave yourself like a reasonable being, you will enjoy yourself, and we shall make a man of you before we are done with you. You can go to bed when you are ready to do so."

The principal retired from the room, and Bates secured the door. It had hardly been closed before Tom began to kick against the wall of the adjoining room. Then he set up a hideous series of yells, that would have done credit to the lungs of wild Indians. He upset the table, and then began to smash the furniture. Crash after crash followed, until it was evident that all the furniture was in process of destruction.

"Bates," called the principal, "take all the furniture out of the brig."

In less than five minutes the old salt reported that he had obeyed the order, and he was directed to unfasten the door of Tom's room. The occupant was still smashing the furniture, and was engaged in tearing the bedstead to pieces.

"Remove him to the brig, Bates," continued the principal, as mildly as though Tom had been a mile from the dormitory.

When the door opened, Tom was stupid enough to suppose that he had carried his point by the racket he had made. He suspended his operations on the bed, from which he had removed the mattress, and was taking out the slats.

"Have you got enough of it?" demanded he, furiously, as Bates entered the room.

The quartermaster made no reply, but took the prisoner by the collar. Tom pitched into him, and struck at him with his fists. Bates bore him to the floor, and then tied his hands behind him. Taking him by the arm, he walked him to the other end of the hall. Tom had heard of the brig, in some of his talks with the boys of the school. It was lighted from the outside, and its walls were as black as a cloudy night.

The old salt made no remark of any kind, but thrust his prisoner into the apartment. He removed the cord with which he had bound him, and then closed and fastened the door. The principal visited the rooms of each of the ruffians, and gave them the same information he had imparted to their leader. If they were disposed to resist, they were more prudent than Tom; and they appeared to accept the situation.

The brig to which Tom had been consigned was a strong room. The walls and ceiling were covered with spruce plank, and these were sheathed with sheet iron. The furniture was of iron, but this had been removed. The interior had been painted black, and it was gloomy enough to answer for a state-prison in the days of feudalism. The windows were strongly barred with iron, and so was the aperture through which the room was lighted at night.

Tom Topover looked about him. There was no furniture to smash. He began to kick against the walls. He followed this with the most unearthly yells. Outside, no attention was paid these sounds, and the prisoner was permitted to wear himself out with his fruitless exertions.

When the principal had informed the other three that they were members of the school, and that they would be well treated if they behaved well, he went to his house. Bates was to sleep in the dormitory, where he had a room for occasional use. Mr. Bristol went to his cottage. Tom continued to kick and pound upon the walls of his prison, till the patience of Bates was somewhat tried, for he wanted to go to sleep. Then the old salt went up-stairs to his room ; and, on the way, he extinguished the lamp which lighted the brig, and Tom was in total darkness. Bates went to bed, and in spite of the racket went to sleep.

For a full hour longer, Tom kept up his demonstrations, until he had tired himself out; and then he ceased. He began to be sleepy, but there was no bed in the room. He seemed to think, that, when he wanted any thing, some one would come to supply him with what he desired. He shouted

with all his might, that he wanted to go to bed.
But the quartermaster slept on till the sun rose
the next morning. Tom slept a little on the hard
iron floor, and he was but little rested in the
morning.

Bates turned out with the sun, and walked
through the hall. He heard nothing, and he went
about his customary duties. At seven o'clock,
breakfast was carried to the prisoners by the old
sailor, who simply put the trays on the tables, and
retired without saying a word, refusing to answer
any questions. Tom was supplied through an
opening in the wall, which was provided with an
iron door. Tom wanted to know how long he
was to stay in this hole, but Bates did not answer
him.

After breakfast, Captain Gildrock visited the
homes of Ben Sinker and Rag Spinner. Neither
of them had been home that night, and their
parents were not a little worried about them.
The principal informed them in regard to the
events of the day before, and then proposed to
admit them to his school. Both fathers and
mothers were glad to have them admitted, and
signed the papers without any hesitation.

"But I don't know where they are," said Mr. Sinker, who was a journeyman carpenter. "I will find my boy if I can, and bring him over to you."

Captain Gildrock had hardly reached his home, after transacting some business in the town, before both the fathers of the truant ruffians called upon him. A man who had been fishing near the mouth of the river had seen the boys come down in a boat with a man. On the lake the boat had set her sail, and gone to the northward. They thought the boat belonged in Burlington, and that the boys had gone there.

"You can go to your work, and I will find them," replied the principal.

"We have no work," said Mr. Sinker, speaking for himself and Mr. Spinner, who was also a journeyman carpenter.

"I am going to Burlington in the Sylph this forenoon; and, if you choose, you can go in her."

About ten o'clock, Captain Gildrock visited the dormitory. Bates reported that three of the boys had given him no trouble, and that Tom was quiet since morning. The prisoners were taken from their rooms, and marched to the steamer.

CHAPTER XV.

FIRST LESSONS IN DISCIPLINE.

CAPTAIN GILDROCK had business in Burlington; and it was more convenient for him to go by the Sylph than by rail, as then he could return when he pleased. Besides, the cool air of the lake was very enjoyable in the hot weather. It required at least three persons to manage her, which took the greater part of the home force; and the principal did not care to leave the prisoners in the dormitory when so many of them were absent.

He expected to have a great deal of trouble with them; and he thought that the sooner he brought them into a state of subjection, the better it would be for the new pupils, and the better for the school. When the family went with him, the cook, and one or two of the domestics, who enjoyed these excursions, were taken, and housekeeping was carried on aboard the yacht.

Tom Topover had passed a very uncomfortable night in the brig, with nothing but a sheet-iron floor to sleep upon. When he was brought out of his dungeon by Bates, who was the turnkey on such occasions, he looked a good deal the worse for the wear. The other three had been more sensible, and had slept very well. The uniform of the steamer had been carried into their rooms, and three of them had put it on; but Tom refused to do so. They had all been supplied with a good breakfast; and, taken separately, all but Tom were disposed to submit. They walked quietly to the yacht when Bates told them what they were to do. Tom did not make any forcible resistance, but he was still stubborn and sullen.

The principal was on the forecastle when they arrived. He looked at them, and saw that three of them had put on the uniform, which indicated that they were in a better frame of mind. He spoke to these three, and told them they were to be part of the ship's company, and would do duty as deck-hands. If they were willing and tractable, they would be treated as well as any students of the school. They said nothing, and the principal did not ask them to make any promises. He preferred to judge them by what they did, rather than by what they said.

"I see that you have not yet put on the new uniform, Thomas Topover," said the principal, approaching the chief of the ruffians.

"I ain't going to put on any uniform!" growled Tom in reply. "I don't belong to the school, and I ain't going to join it."

"If you want to knock your head against solid walls of stone and iron, you will have the privilege of doing so until you are tired of it; for you will not hurt the walls, and you will hurt your head — Bates," called the captain.

The old salt presented himself; and the principal directed him to tie the hands of Tom behind him, and confine him to a stanchion.

"I ain't going to be tied up any more!" protested Tom.

But Bates proceeded to obey the order just as though he had said nothing. The prisoner had lost a great deal of the pluck he exhibited the night before, and his opposition was very feeble.

His three companions looked on while he was secured: they did not say he was a fool to kick when it did no good, but they thought so.

"When you are ready to put on your uniform, and act like a reasonable being, you will be released, and be allowed to join your companions," said the principal curtly.

"You haven't any right to tie me up in this way, and I won't stand it," grumbled Tom.

"I will take care of that part of the business, and will settle the question of my right with any one who disputes it," added Captain Gildrock. "As long as you choose to be obstinate, and refuse to put on your uniform, you will remain in your present condition. When you want to put on your uniform and do your duty, you have only to say so, and you will be set at liberty, as your companions are."

Perhaps these last words were said quite as much for the benefit of Spinner and Sinker, the fathers of the two missing boys, who had just come on board. They saw three of the four prisoners on duty, for they were sweeping up the deck. They hardly knew them in their new uniform.

"That's the right way to serve them," said Spinner to the principal. "I hope you will make my boy mind, for I don't have time to look out for him when I have work."

"The one thing required of the boys, above all others, is, that they shall obey orders," replied Captain Gildrock. "If they do that, and try to discharge their duty, they will be all right here; for I give them plenty of recreation, and provide them with the means to be happy and contented."

The steamer backed away from the wharf, and commenced her trip down Beechwater. Bates remained on the forecastle; and when he found that the three boys were willing to obey, or that they did obey, whether they were willing or not, he did not give them any hard work to do. He limbered up his tongue, and began to explain their duties to them. In spite of themselves, they were interested.

He took them to all parts of the steamer, and pointed out the lines they were to handle in making fast to a wharf. He showed them how the boats were lowered into the water, and manned, and gave them all the instruction they could digest. Kidd Digfield was not willing to confess it, but he found that he rather liked life on board of a steamer.

When he had finished his lesson, the quarter-master went on deck to report to Captain Gildrock, that the three boys were as tame as kittens, and he did not think there would be any trouble with them. The captain was not at all confident that this would be the case, and asked Bates if he had left them alone; suggesting that they might release Tom, and take to one of the boats, which he had instructed them how to put into the water.

"I want Kidd Digfield and Nim Splugger to say a word or two to Tom, and I have given them a chance to do so," replied Bates. "They will tell him that he is a fool to resist."

"Perhaps they will," added the principal, with a smile.

"I know they will, and Tom will ask to put on the uniform in less than half an hour," persisted Bates.

And he was right. The old man had had a great deal of experience, and could form some idea of what the young ruffians were thinking about. He went to the ladder, and looked down to the forecastle, without allowing them to see him. As he supposed they would, they went to Tom as soon as they saw that they were alone. But Tom had been the first to speak.

"You are the three biggest fools I ever saw!" he muttered, as they walked towards him. "What did you cave in for? You are acting like so many spring chickens."

"What would you have us do?" asked Kidd, with a broad grin; for he felt that he ought to apologize for his submission, when his chief had resisted to the utmost.

"If you would do as I do, they would soon get sick of it, and let us go," replied Tom.

"It's no use to buck your head against a stone wall. You don't hurt the wall any, as the captain says; and you do hurt your head," replied Nim Splugger. "We are going to take things easy till we have a good chance to do something, and then we are going to do it."

"That's the best way," added Kidd. "They think we have given in, and treat us very well."

"We had a good bed last night, and every thing was nice. If we had done as you did, we should have had to sleep on the floor," argued Nim.

"But I won't stand it."

"You can't help yourself, Tom."

The chief had begun to weaken. Even if he wanted to escape, the best way was to do as his companions had done. When Bates had allowed them time enough to consider the matter, he came below. Tom at once asked him for the uniform. He was released, and taken to a stateroom, from which he soon came out dressed like his companions. His duties were explained to him, and he listened in sullen silence.

The day was very pleasant, with scarcely any wind; and, when the Sylph had passed Split Rock, Dory discovered a sailboat trying to get ahead in the light breeze. With the glass, he discovered that it contained a man and two boys. Paul Bristol was doing duty as wheelman, and he was sent to the principal to report the fact.

The boat had scarcely a particle of wind, and had not yet made half the distance to Burlington. The two boys, Rag Spinner and Ben Sinker, had been broiling in the hot sun all the forenoon; and they were willing enough to accept the invitation to go on board of the steamer, though without understanding the reason for the request. The man in the boat asked to be taken in tow; but Captain Gildrock ordered the Sylph to go ahead, without heeding the request.

Raglan Spinner was not a little astonished to find his father on board of the steamer, and Ben Sinker was hardly less surprised. At the next glance they saw their companions of the day before dressed in the uniform of the Industrial School, and this was a still greater surprise. They began to see why they had been invited to go on board of the Sylph.

"So you were going to run away, Raglan, were you?" said Mr. Spinner sternly, as he confronted his son. "Why didn't you come home last night?"

"I didn't like to after the scrape we got into yesterday," pleaded Rag, with a laugh; and it was apparent that he did not stand in awe of his father.

"I have put you where I can find you when I want you," continued the carpenter. "You will spend the next three years in the care of Captain Gildrock."

"All right: we shall have plenty of boating," replied the boy.

The two boys were immediately supplied with a uniform, and took their places with the other Topovers on the forecastle. Bates proceeded to go over his instructions for deck-hands again, for the benefit of the new-comers.

Before they reached Burlington the principal shot a duck on the wing, and the bird dropped into the water. The steamer was stopped, and the captain gave the order for the port-quarter boat to be put into the water, and the bird secured. Under the direction of Bates, the deck-hands had an opportunity to apply the knowledge they had gained. The original Topovers were ordered to the thwarts, and Bates acted as coxswain. The bird was dead, and not likely to escape; so that the officer in charge of the boat did not hurry himself. He took time to instruct his pupils in pulling a man-of-war stroke; and, before they reached the duck, they did tolerably well, for they had learned to row before.

When the steamer reached her destination, she did not go up to a wharf as usual; but the order was given to let go the anchor just outside of the breakwater. The principal, with a smile, said it would be cooler here than at the wharf, while those on board were waiting for him. The boat was dropped into the water again, and the same crew pulled the captain to the shore. While he was attending to the business of the bank, of which he was a director, Bates gave his pupils a lesson in managing the boat, and handling the oars. In an hour the principal was ready to go on board, and the steamer returned to Genverres.

CHAPTER XVI.

THE PUPILS FOR THE NEXT YEAR.

AS soon as the fathers of the last two recruits to the school had been landed, the Sylph went out to the lake again, and started on a long cruise, from which she did not return till after dark. The principal went ashore at Plattsburgh, and the boys took some more lessons in rowing.

At dinner and supper on this day, the Topovers were seated with the family, and were not required to sit at a second table. On the return, Kidd Digfield was sent to the pilot-house to take a lesson in steering, for any of the deck-hands were liable to be called upon to act as wheelmen. The reprobate was not willing to confess that he was delighted with this occupation, even though he had to act under the orders of Dory Dornwood.

He soon got the hang of the wheel; and because

he was interested in his occupation, in spite of his efforts to appear otherwise, he was an apt scholar. It was not a difficult thing to learn, as long as a course was given to him; and he soon felt quite at home at the wheel.

"I rather like this thing," said Kidd, when he joined his associates on the lower deck. "I have steered the steamer nearly all the way since we left Plattsburgh."

"You are a traitor, Kidd Digfield!" was the reply with which the chief Topover received this manifestation of pride on the part of one of his band. "You will give us all away."

"What do you mean by traitor, Tom Topover?" demanded Kidd.

"Do you think I would let Dory Dornwood boss me?" growled Tom.

"He is the captain of the steamer; and I would rather have him boss me in the steamer, than have you do it in a sailboat, for he knows what he is about every time."

"All right! You have gone over to the enemy."

"What's the use to talk about bossing, Tom?" interposed Nim Splugger. "You want to be boss all the time; and, in a boat, you are ten times as rough with a fellow as Dory Dornwood. He is as polite as a dancing-master."

"Then you are going to leave me to fight this thing out alone?" demanded Tom, disgusted with the admissions of his friends. "You don't catch me bending my knee to Dory Dornwood."

"He don't ask any fellow to bend his knee to him. He shows you how to do a thing, and don't bully, like you do, Tom," added Kidd.

"If you think more of him than you do of me, you can throw me over," added Tom, with a show of meekness." "But I thought you were going to make the best of it till we had a good chance to make a strike."

"I am making the best of it, and I am getting along first-rate," added Kidd, as he turned upon his heel and walked away.

"When there is a chance to do any thing, you will find us there," added Nim Splugger. "But I think you are making a fool of yourself, by setting your teeth even against things you like. I have had a first-rate time to-day, and we are living as well as we should at the hotel."

"And when you go on shore you will be locked

into a room with iron bars on the windows," sneered Tom.

"The room has a good bed, and every thing a fellow wants in it. The lock and the bars don't hurt me, but they will not be kept up a great while. I didn't expect to like it; but I do like it, and we are having plenty of fun every hour in the day."

"I don't want to cave in, but I like this thing as well as Kidd and Nim," added Pell Sankland.

"It is vacation now, and we are doing nothing but play with this steamer. What will you do when you are set down to your books, or made to shove a foreplane all the afternoon?" asked Tom, with the curl of disgust hanging about his lips still.

"What did we build the Thunderer for?" demanded Nim sharply.

"For fun, of course. We shouldn't have done it if it had been hard work."

"All the tools we had were a shingling-hatchet, a bucksaw, and a half-inch auger; and we worked for a week for the fun of it!" exclaimed Nim warmly. "Do you think there will be any less fun in working three or four hours in the afternoon with good tools, and machinery to help us?"

"It's no use to talk with you, Nim Splugger. You have sold out," replied Tom. "You want to be under Dory Dornwood's thumb; and you may do it if you like, I shall not."

"You will be under his thumb just as much as I am, whether you like it or not; and if you want to get licked into doing what you are told, like a contrary horse, you can do it if you like," answered Nim, as he turned on his heel, as his companion had done, and left the impracticable leader.

"Those fellows don't like to study their lessons any better than I do, and I guess they will have enough of it here," added Tom.

"We can all read, write, and cipher; and we don't have to study such things as we did at the town-school," replied Pell Sankland.

"I am not going to stay in this school any longer than I can help. As soon as I get a chance, I shall be among the missing, though all the rest of the fellows have deserted me," added Tom.

"I don't believe in kicking at nothing, Tom," argued Pell. "It only wrenches a fellow's foot.

We have all had a good time since we were raked in, and I don't believe in making a row as long as things go well with us. You don't get such roast beef as we had for dinner to-day when you are at home, nor such puddings and pies."

"The grub is good enough, but I would rather be free than to be well fed. I must have my liberty."

"We have liberty enough for me on board of this steamer," said Pell, as in turn he, too, turned on his heel, and left the chief to his own reflections.

Tom Topover was restored to the room in which he had first been placed; and he had a good bed, though he was locked in, and the iron bars confronted him at the windows. As the recruits were not outwardly refractory, they were taken to the table in the house, with the others of the principal's family; for he regarded his students as a part of his family, and treated them as such.

Every day during the week the Sylph was moving about the lake. In conformity with his new idea, the principal was notifying the parents of the new pupils he had decided to accept for the term of the coming year. They were all the sons of poor people, and some of them were quite as hard boys as Tom Topover. In fact, he had selected them because they were not controllable by their parents and teachers. The Beech-Hill School was to assume the character, in part, of a reformatory institution.

The half of the school that remained over were in excellent discipline, and would give the principal no trouble. Three days before the term was to begin, there were still six vacancies in the roll, and the principal was in doubt. Just at this time he received a visit from the six young firemen, as he called them to distinguish them from the rest of the Topovers, with whom they had been associated. The principal was rather surprised to see them. He had learned from his sister, that they had been actively employed in rendering assistance to the Widow Sankland since the fire, not only in soliciting articles of clothing and food for them, but in sawing and splitting her wood, and doing other chores about the house. Two of them had even spent three days in taking care of the children when she was at work; for the fire, and the "advertising" it had given her, had brought her a considerable increase of customers.

" Well, boys, what can I do for you this time ? " asked the principal, with a pleasant smile ; for he was very kindly disposed towards them since he had heard of their good deeds.

" We are almost sorry that we were not captured with the rest of the Topovers, in the Goldwing," said Ash Burton, with a smile, to indicate that he did not quite mean what he said.

"If you had been, perhaps I should have prosecuted the whole of you," replied the captain, pleasantly. "But I don't quite understand the force of your remark."

" Tom Topover and the rest of them have been rewarded for their part in the affair by being admitted as pupils of the Beech-Hill Industrial School," continued Ash. "If we had been caught in the boat, and stuck to the lies Tom told, we might have been admitted also."

" Rewarded ? " exclaimed Captain Gildrock. " They have been close prisoners since they were admitted. They are locked into their rooms at night, and the windows are protected with iron bars. Do you call that rewarding them ? "

"I shouldn't care any thing about the barred windows if I could only be admitted," said Sam

Spottwood. "I don't say that if stealing a boat is the way to get in, we shall try to get in that way; but some other fellows might say so."

"But all four of the original Topovers fought with all their might against the discipline, till we brought them to terms; and I am sure they do not consider their admission as a reward, but as a severe punishment, even worse than being brought up before a court."

"They have been in the school over a week, sir: do they still keep up the fight?" asked Ash.

"No: they have had enough of it, and are behaving very well," replied the principal thoughtfully.

"We have talked the matter over among ourselves, and with our parents. We all agree that the Topovers were lucky to get into the school, and we all wish we were in their shoes."

"Then I will admit you all," replied Captain Gildrock.

"Will you indeed, sir? We will not give you any trouble, and we won't run away if you don't lock us up nights!" exclaimed Sam.

The boys went home to inform their parents of the good news. They were all the children of parents who could not afford to pay their tuition in any school, whatever they might learn there; and, in this respect, they were within the rule the principal had laid down for his guidance. He had been thinking over this question of admission that day. He had already decided to receive ten refractory boys, and he thought this would be enough to enable him to try the question of reform.

He was not pleased with the statement that he had rewarded the Topovers by receiving them, and he was willing to do something to remove such a mistaken impression in the community. The ranks of both classes were full now, and he had only to think of the actual work of the first term. Before the end of the last week, the instructors arrived; and they were not especially pleased when they learned the character of some of the new scholars.

The principal explained his new idea to them, and they were willing to co-operate with him in carrying out his purpose. Mr. Brookbine, the master carpenter, was a disciplinarian himself; and he did not object to the original Topovers, or to the hard boys from Whitehall, Plattsburgh, and Burlington. He was confident that he could make them work. If they did not take kindly to the use of tools, he would set them to lugging lumber, or something of that sort, till they got over their sulkiness.

"As we used to say in the navy, we must keep every thing 'all taut,' and we shall get along very well," said the principal.

CHAPTER XVII.

TOM TOPOVER FINDS HIMSELF IGNORED.

ON the first day of the new term, Captain Gild-rock made his usual speech of welcome and explanation. Just one-half of the school were new scholars, and it took a week to get them properly classified. Nearly one-third of the number were "hard boys;" though six of them had been disciplined for two weeks, on board of the steamer. But the new pupils had not learned their duties in the schoolroom.

Tom Topover had come to that part of the programme of the institution, where he expected to recover his lost prestige as a leader of his gang. Study had always been an abomination to him; and he supposed it was to his companions, the original Topovers. For himself, he refused to make any effort to apply himself; and, when called upon for a recitation, he was entirely unprepared. He thought he could get the better of his teachers and the principal in this department.

Mr. Darlingby sent him to his room to learn his lesson when he failed. Tom laughed in his sleeve, at this sort of discipline. He stretched himself on the bed, and went to sleep. At dinner-time his meal consisted of nothing but bread and butter, and cold water. Tom did not touch it; for he was disgusted with such food, after the good living he had so greatly enjoyed since he came to the school.

Kidd Digfield and the others did the best they could with their lessons, and were subjected to no discipline on account of them. They had been to the grammar school, and were fair scholars in the ordinary branches. No difficult tasks were assigned to them, and they passed the forenoon with infinitely better satisfaction to themselves than they had expected.

In the afternoon, when the students were as-sembled in the shops, they all felt more at home. They were provided with tools, all in good order, and required to make a box two feet long, a foot wide, and eight inches deep. This was the work of all the new boys; and the use of the tools was explained to them, precisely as it had been to all the classes who had preceded them.

All of them, wherever they came from, took kindly to this lesson. It was a new thing to most of them, even to those who had some little skill in tinkering. Kidd Digfield declared at night, when the shopwork was finished, that he had had a first-rate time. In fact, he and his companions, with the exception of Tom, were fairly reconstructed. It was nothing but fun to make a box, with such excellent tools as they were provided with; and they laughed when they thought of the bungling work they had done on the Thunderer.

After supper, there was still an hour and a half of daylight, and the barges were manned with their new crews. One of them was assigned to the new pupils for the first lessons, and Dory Dornwood was to act as coxswain. But Captain Gildrock was in the Marian, with a crew of five of the old boys; and he kept near enough to quell a rebellion if one should break out. But this was fun for the boys; and they were instructed according to the man-of-war rules, rather than those of the sporting fraternity.

Tom Topover, from the grated window of his chamber, saw his companions in the boats, and wished he were with them. It had not occurred to him that he was to be deprived of his air and exercise, and be kept in his room after the closing of the study-hours. He realized now, that he was to be kept a prisoner in his room, on bread and water, until he learned his lesson.

He had some mechanical taste; and he had looked forward, with something like pleasure, to the time when he should be required to handle the tools in the shop. Enough had been said among the boys in regard to this part of their daily duties to inspire his ambition, and he expected to distinguish himself in this department. On Saturday the ship's company of the Sylph was to be organized, as it had been in the two preceding years; but the lessons came first.

The supper of the prisoner was the same as his dinner had been. He was so faint, that he ate his allowance, and drank the glass of water that came with the food; but he did it with a rebellious soul. In the evening he heard the voices of his companions about the dormitory. The excited speech and the noisy laugh in the adjoining rooms, as his late associates talked over the experiences of the day, indicated that they were all happy. But no one went near him after he had eaten his supper. As he listened to the sounds which came to him, he heard his friends say that the bars had been removed from the windows of their rooms sometime during the day.

In fact, Tom's three cronies were on precisely the same footing now as even the older pupils of the school. They were not locked into their rooms that night; for they had accepted the situation, and were doing all that was required of them in a cheerful spirit. In the boat, Dory Dornwood had instructed them in the use of the oars; but he had done it so pleasantly and politely, that they could not find a word of fault with him.

It was plain to Tom, that his friends had surrendered without conditions; though they still said they were acting only from motives of policy. It was no use, they continued to say, to buck their heads against a stone wall. It was easier to do their duty than it was to rebel, and take the consequences.

At about dark the rebellious chief heard the

voices of his cronies in the next room, which was Kidd Digfield's. The discipline had been relaxed in their favor, for they had not before been allowed to visit one another's rooms. They did not talk about him: he had not heard his name mentioned by them. He felt very lonely, and very much hurt by the want of loyalty to him on their part. He rapped several times on the wall. It was more to see if they would notice his signal than for any other reason.

Kidd knocked on the wall, in reply to the call. Tom asked him to come to the door, and speak to him through the keyhole. Kidd replied that he could not do it, they were forbidden to have any communication with him. This he said loud enough to be heard by the prisoner. He did not care who else heard him, though he suspected that Bates could not be far off.

The answer roused the anger of the bully, and he began to use some strong language. Nim Splugger advised Kidd not to make any reply. This increased Tom's wrath; and he called them traitors, so that his voice could be heard half the length of the hall. Then, in his anger, he resorted to kicking against the wall again. This soon brought Bates. The door was unlocked; and, without a word of any kind, the old salt collared him, and marched him to the brig. The furniture had not been restored to its place, and he was left alone in the iron-bound cell.

To Tom Topover, the most galling feature of the discipline was in the fact that no notice had been taken of him. Even his companions would have no intercourse with him. He was shut up in the brig, and as fully ignored as though he had been dead and buried. But he had decided not to study his lessons, and he could not give up. He spent a miserable night in the gloom of the dark prison. His breakfast was brought to him in the morning, but it was the same as his dinner and his supper the day before. Without a word of explanation, he was conducted back to his chamber, and locked into it. The book he had brought from the schoolroom was there.

All he had to do in order to end his term of imprisonment, was to learn the lesson assigned to him. The book was a simple treatise on natural philosophy. He was not required to commit any thing to memory, only to read over the first half-dozen pages. It was simply a question of will.

He had refused even to look into the book. No one came near him during the forenoon, and he hardly heard a sound. His slices of bread and butter, and his glass of water, came to him at noon.

"How long have I got to stand this thing?" asked Tom, in a tone of utter disgust, when Bates put his dinner on the table.

The old man made no reply to him, and would not even look at him. He would not come again till supper-time; and Tom saw that he must back down then, or there would be no chance to do so before night. But he had not the moral courage to say he would learn his lesson. When the door was locked upon him, he picked up the book; but, before he had looked into it, he began to cry, though he was a great fellow of fifteen. It took him an hour to get over this feeling of depression, and then he looked into the book. He began to read the lesson which had been assigned to him.

It was simple reading, and about matters within his comprehension. Before he realized that he was actually engaged in learning the lesson assigned to .him, he was interested in the subject. It had been chosen for this reason, — that he could hardly help enjoying what he read. He found a solace in the book during the afternoon; and, when his supper was brought to him, he informed Bates that he had learned his lesson. The old man did not say a word, even to hint that he heard him; but, in a few minutes, Mr. Darlingby appeared. He had nothing to say on the question of discipline, but took the book at once, and proceeded to examine Tom on the first pages. The rebellious pupil was well posted in every thing he had read, and had studied far beyond the task assigned to him.

All the instructor did when he had finished the recitation, was to inform him that he was at liberty to leave his room. He made no remarks, did not preach to him, or even point a moral from the events of his imprisonment. Tom went out of the room, and descended the stairs. The students were just coming out of the mansion after their supper, and they were hurrying to the boathouse. Tom showed himself among them; but not one of them manifested any surprise at seeing him, or said a word to him about his conduct.

All this was very strange. He hastened to Kidd Digfield when he saw him coming, and was thinking how he should explain to his crony the fact that he had given in. He had yielded, and that was a thing he was not in the habit of doing; and he felt that some apology was necessary to atone for his wickedness.

"We are going to row in the Gildrock," said Kidd, as soon as he saw his defeated chief. "There is a place for you in the boat, Tom."

"All right: I shouldn't mind taking a turn at the oars," replied Tom, as they were joined by Nim and Pell.

"You are No. 11, next to the stroke oar," added Nim.

"I am No. 2," added Pell, as if he was simply recalling the locality of his place in the barge.

Not a word about his imprisonment, not a hint in relation to their opinion of his conduct. Tom thought it was very strange. He was allowed to take his place in the ranks of the students, and no one seemed to know that he had been standing out against orders. The same state of things had bothered delinquents in years before, and they could not explain it. Others could, if they had been disposed to do so.

The principal had requested all the pupils not

to allude to any matters of discipline to offenders. If one had been punished, they were not to talk about the matter, and not to inform the delinquent that they even knew of the fact. To the reformed Topovers, it seemed more like a good joke on Tom not to notice what had happened; and they took pleasure in complying with the principal's request. He had made quite a speech in regard to this matter. Tom's vanity had no standing-room. Nobody seemed to care whether he had been punished or not.

CHAPTER XVIII.

NAUTICAL INSTRUCTION ON THE WHARF.

THE first two weeks of the term were devoted to giving the new students a proper start in their studies, and in the work of the shop. At the same time they learned to pull an oar, and to handle a rowboat. At the end of that time the crew of the Winooski could pull a very fair stroke, and were tolerably obedient to the orders of the coxswain. A Whitehall fellow undertook to have his own way at one time, and the boat went to the shore at once. In five minutes more he was locked up in his room.

The next day, after he had backed down, and resumed his place in the schoolroom, he took his oar again. No one appeared to know that he had disobeyed orders; no one said any thing; he received no sympathy, and was subjected to no condemnation, among his associates. He had a good chance to turn over a new leaf if he was disposed to do so. The very fact that he was ignored, proved that his fellow-students were in full sympathy with the principal.

The students were simply requested to ignore any offender, and they could disregard the request if they were desirous of doing so. If there was any real or fancied grievance among the pupils, of course they would disregard it; but just now all was serene, and even the bad boys were delighted with the routine of the institution. The early lessons were given out with a view to interest them. In the shop, they were set to making something,—a box at first,—which could not help amusing them.

On the first Saturday of the term the ship's company of the Sylph were organized. Dory Dornwood was captain again; though only for the first month, while the new scholars were broken in. It was understood that Oscar Chester was to take his place from the first of October. The principal offices were filled by the old students, who were qualified to instruct their subordinates. The recruits were scattered about: some were firemen, some were stewards, and most of them were deck-hands.

The day was devoted to exercising the students in their new duties. Of course, there was considerable friction in places, but not so much as the principal had expected. As long as the boys tried to do their duty, their short-comings and their failures were overlooked. If one refused to obey an order, he was shut up in a storeroom; and excellent discipline prevailed on the second Saturday, when the practice was repeated.

On the following Monday afternoon, all hands were ordered to the boat-house after dinner, in place of going to the shops. The Lily, which the students had built in the earlier part of the year, had been brought alongside of the wharf by Bates and Mr. Bristol. The work of rigging the boat was to be begun at this time. On the wharf lay the two masts of the schooner, which had been made in Burlington, and brought down a few days before. There were several other sticks on the wharf, whose use most of the students did not understand. Lying on the top of the masts were a great number of small pieces of rope; and old Bates was as busy as a bee, with a lot of things which were incomprehensible to even the old students.

The principal was the instructor on the present occasion; for, of the subjects to be treated, the other teachers were as ignorant as the pupils. The boys were requested to seat themselves on the spars and timbers. Captain Gildrock picked out one of the pieces of rope about three feet long, from the pile, and then mounted a box where he could be seen by all hands; and several of the teachers were present.

"The next business in order is to rig the boat we have built," he began. "It is not a very complicated matter to rig a fore-and-aft schooner."

"What does that mean?" asked Sax Coburg, one of the hard fellows from Burlington, though he was interested in rigging the boat.

"I will tell you in a moment, when I have spoken of the general plan of proceeding while we are rigging the boat," replied the principal, who encouraged the pupils in asking sensible questions. "It is a comparatively simple matter to rig a schooner; but, in connection with it, I shall endeavor to have you learn something of the rig of other kinds of vessels. Those of you who live on Lake Champlain never see any sailing craft on its waters, except schooners and sloops. Now, may I ask some student to tell me what a ship is, as he understands it?"

Most of the boys thought they knew all about it, and raised their hands to indicate that they wished to speak, as they had been instructed to do.

"Bark Duxbury," said the principal, calling upon one of the old boys of the school.

"A vessel with three masts," replied the student called.

"Is that the entire definition?"

"It is all the definition I know," replied Bark.

"What do you say, Leo Pownall?"

"A vessel with three masts and square-rigged," answered Leo.

"What's square-rigged?" interposed Jack Dumper.

"Raise your hand if you wish to ask a question; but no question should be put in the midst of one subject, which relates to another, till a fit time comes to do so," said the principal. "Leo Pownall is nearer right than Bark was, but the definition is not accurate. I dare say you could all give an opinion, and I should like to hear you all on the subject if I had more time. A ship is a vessel with three masts, square-rigged on the fore, main, and mizzen masts. You cannot correctly define a ship in less words."

At this point Jack Dumper raised his hand again, and the principal indicated that he would hear him. He said he did not know what a ship was, for the reason that he did not know what square-rigged meant. This time Captain Gildrock approved the question, and nodded to Mr. Jepson, who planted a large easel on a box near the one on which the principal stood. He placed on it a great pile of large papers; and, of course, the attention of the pupils was strongly attracted to what was coming.

"The eye must help the ear in this lesson," said the principal, as he turned over the paper on the top of the pile. It was a picture of a ship under full sail. "This is a full-rigged ship," said he.

When the students had looked at it a minute or two, he selected another paper, and placed it on the easel so that it could be seen by all.

"This is a fore-and-aft schooner. What difference do you notice between the two vessels?" he asked.

"The ship is square-rigged, and the schooner is not," replied Fred Grafton, when the captain pointed to him.

"Right: one has yards, and the other has not;" and half a dozen hands were raised, before the words were fairly out of his mouth. "What are yards? is the question you wish to ask," continued the principal, as he exhibited the picture of the ship again. "The sticks across the masts are yards; and the sails are hung down from them, like the banner of the engine-company on parade. A schooner of this kind," added the principal, as he presented the schooner again, "has no yards on her masts."

"I see it!" exclaimed Jack Dumper, with enthusiam.

"I am glad you do; but you need not take the trouble to mention it," added Captain Gildrock, with a smile. "Now, your eye has taught you the difference between a full-rigged ship and a fore-and-aft schooner. One has yards, and the other has no yards. Here is another vessel with three masts."

The picture was displayed on the easel, and a few of the boys put up their hands to indicate that they knew what to call her.

"What is it, Pinkler?"

"A bark."

"Why a bark?"

"Because she is not square-rigged on her hind-mast," replied Archie Pinkler.

"Hind-mast is rather rough to a nautical ear," said the principal, "but you are right. Fore, main, and mizzen mast are the proper names; and you had better begin now to use these terms. I heard a young lady singing the other day, ' My bark is on the wave! '   Did she mean this kind of a vessel?"

Some of the older students laughed, and some were puzzled. The question looked as though there was a catch under it, and they were shy about answering it.

" We read in the Good Book, about those 'who go down to the sea in ships.'   Does it mean square-rigged on the fore, main, and mizzen masts? We find in the New Testament frequent allusions to the ships on the Lake of Galilee. Were these square-rigged vessels?"

"They were nothing but boats," replied Tucker Prince, when his name was called. "The word ship and bark are used, in a general sense, to mean any kind of a vessel."

"That is entirely correct, Prince.— How many fingers have you, Kidder Digfield?" asked the principal.

"Eight, sir," replied the ex-Topover, with a grin.

"I have ten, and I am apparently more fortunate than you are; but I use the word fingers in a general sense. When you come down to particulars, you say, very properly, that you have eight fingers."

"I don't think thumbs are fingers," added Kidd, when the principal nodded to him.

"All right: you have a perfect right to your own opinion. How many toes have you?"

"Ten."

"But two of them are big toes. Why not say that you have eight toes and two big toes?" added the captain. "Now you know what a ship is, and that the word is used, in a general sense, to mean any kind of vessel. We speak of the ship's company, in general terms, on board of a craft of any size. The ocean and coast steamers are called ships, and some of the former have four masts. A few sailing-ships, like the Great Republic, have been rigged with four masts.

"What do they call the after-mast when there are four?" asked Dick Short.

"The usage differs somewhat: some call it the jigger-mast, and those of more dignity call it the after-mizzen-mast. In a vessel with two masts, the terms are main and mizzen mast. I have shown you a ship and a bark; what is this?" asked the captain, as he displayed another picture.

"A brig," replied Con Bunker; though none spoke unless they were called upon.

"Right; and what is a brig, properly defined?"

"A vessel with two masts, square-rigged on both," replied Hop Cabright.

"What is this?" and the principal showed another drawing.

Such a craft had never been seen on the lake; and only Matt Randolph, and a few others from New York and Boston, could answer.

"It is a three-masted schooner," answered Tucker Prince. "Her masts have the same names as those of a ship."

"And she is a fore-and-after," added Captain Gildrock.

The next picture was a puzzle to all except Matt Randolph.

CHAPTER XIX.

THE DIFFERENT RIGS OF VESSELS.

"WELL, Randolph, you seem to be the only one who can give the name of a vessel with this rig," said Captain Gildrock, calling upon the New-Yorker.

"She is a barkentine," replied Matt. "The rig is new, and the name has not yet got into the dictionary."

"And I hope it will not get there as you pronounce it, and as the newspapers usually spell it," added the principal. "The word 'brigantine' is spelled with an a; and there is no reason why it should not be a barkantine, rather than a barkentine."

"But 'bark' was formerly 'barque,' suggested Matt.

"If she were a barquentine, that would be another thing. Some people still insist upon writing a bank 'cheque;' but there are a score of words that might as well be spelled the same way, if the fashion had not changed.— I suppose you have seen four-masted schooners, Matt?"

"Yes, sir, a few of them; though they are not very common," replied the New-Yorker.

"Many of these three-masted schooners are three times as big as a full-rigged ship used to be in old times; and I mean within my recollection. They were first used as coalers, vessels which had to work up Delaware Bay and River; and these schooners could be kept closer to the wind in beating.— What is this?" asked the captain, as he changed the picture.

"A brigantine," replied Lon Dorset when called.

"I think not," added the principal.

"I have heard of a vessel like that, rigged like a ship forward, and like a schooner aft, called a brigantine," persisted Lon.

"So have I; but this is an hermaphrodite brig, though she is sometimes called a brig simply, for short," added Captain Gildrock.

"What is a brigantine, then?" asked Lon.

"It is a rig you seldom, if ever, see in a sailing

vessel in these days; though it is sometimes applied to steamers."

"It is called a small brig, in the dictionary," said Lon.

"Some of the dictionaries are not correct on nautical matters. I should say that a brigantine was a fore-and-main-topsail schooner; that is, a vessel with two masts, fore and aft sails below, and with a topsail and topgallant-sail on each mast. A full-rigged vessel carries a royal above these, and may have a skysail also."

"What is a moon-raker?" asked Thad Glovering with a laugh.

"That is a fancy sail, a term applied to a sail set above the skysail. There is another distinction between a full-rigged mast and that of a schooner. The former is provided with a top, which is wanting in the latter. A brig has a top on each mast, while a schooner or a brigantine has none. A top is a kind of platform, on which several men may stand, in large vessels, over which the futtock shrouds pass," continued the principal, as he pointed it out on the foremast of the vessel in the picture.— "What is this?" he asked, diplaying another drawing.

"A topsail schooner," answered Bent Fillwing.

"She is sometimes called a fore-topsail schooner, but the expression is redundant, since there is no such craft as a main-topsail schooner. She carries a topsail and topgallant-sail on her foremast."

"She would be a brigantine if she had the same rig on her mainmast, without any tops," added Matt Randolph.

"There is only one other craft which we shall notice," continued the principal, changing the drawing. "What is it?"

"A sloop," replied Nat Long. "We have plenty of them on Lake Champlain."

"This is the simplest rig of all. But sloops, especially in yachts, vary a great deal. This is the rig of the English cutter, in the main; though some of them have a couple of yards on the mast, as you never see it in an ordinary sloop. As I have said before, there are many variations in all these rigs. Some vessels are provided with sails which others of the same rig do not have. The fashions change also. A ship now is quite a different thing from what it was forty years ago. The study is to work a vessel with the fewest men that can handle her; for, the less the number, the

smaller the expense, and the more profitable the
the vessel is to her owners.

"For example, mercantile ships, as distinguished
from naval vessels, have a different rig from what
they had twenty-five years ago. Instead of one
large topsail, they have two sails, called the upper
and lower topsails, with an extra yard. It saves
handling the larger sail, and avoids much of the
difficult and dangerous work of reefing in heavy
weather. But you do not see this rig in the navy.
Men-of-war are always heavily manned, and they
have force enough to handle any sail. Now we
will turn to the business of rigging this schooner.
It is better for you to learn the names and the
uses of things as you proceed with the work,
rather than attempt to get at them in a lesson.

"Nautical terms look very formidable to shore-
people; and so they are, in fact, though not so
much so as people generally imagine. There is
a certain system about naming the various spars
and pieces of rigging, which simplifies the whole
subject. In a ship, the three words 'fore,' 'main,'
and 'mizzen' distinguish the fore and aft position
of every thing. For the elevation we have the
word simply; then with the addition of top, top-

gallant, and royal, we fix the position above the deck."

"To indicate the side to which a part belongs, we say weather and lee if the vessel is under way, or starboard and port if she is at rest. The weather - maintop - gallantbrace covers the whole matter. If you know what a brace is, you can describe any similar piece of rigging in the ship. To-morrow afternoon, when some drawings I am having made are done, I shall explain the rigging of a ship.

"I might talk all the afternoon about the rigging of even a fore-and-aft schooner, but I am afraid it would only perplex you. There are at least thirty different kinds of blocks, each with its proper name, indicating its position or use.

"What is a block?" asked Sax Coburg.

"It is a kind of pulley," replied the principal, picking one up from the pile on the wharf. "It consists of a shell, which is the wooden frame, the sheave or wheel, the pin, or axis on which the wheel turns, and the strap, which is the rope or iron by which it is secured to some other body. The sides of a shell, which usually round outward, are called the cheeks. That's all we need say about blocks till we come to use them in setting up the rigging."

"The two round sticks, squared at the top, are the masts. Are they of the same length?"

"These seem to be," replied Luke Bennington, "but the mainmast is generally longer than the foremast."

"These are of the same length. This afternoon we will put them in their places. The first thing to do is to rig the shears. Do you know what they are?"

"Something to cut with — a pair of scissors," replied a shore-boy.

"Not exactly, though it is rigged something like a pair of shears. It is a kind of derrick, used for hoisting heavy weights."

Bates had been at work for some time on a couple of the long round sticks on the wharf, and had lashed them together at a point about three feet from the smaller ends. The students were required to carry this machine to the deck of the Lily; and, after guy-lines had been attached to it, it was raised in the forward part of the deck. A purchase-block had been attached to the lashing, and a single block to one of the arms of the shears above.

A noose was then slipped on the mast just above the centre of gravity, to which the purchase-block was hooked. A couple of lines were fastened to the top of the spar, so that it could be swayed in any direction desired.

"Now we need a snatch-block," said the principal; and Bates immediately brought one from the pile on the wharf. "What is a block for?"

"To increase the effect of the power applied," answered Leo Pownall, who had been called upon as one who would be likely to know.

"Is that so?" asked the principal, looking around among the students.

"No, sir," replied one indicated. "The power is gained only with movable blocks."

"It takes ten pounds to balance the same weight by a line passed over a single fixed pulley, or through a block," continued the principal. "You gain nothing except at the expense of time. If you pull one rope down a foot, the other is raised only a foot. With a movable pulley, you have to pull down two feet to raise the weight one foot. With one pound of power, you raise two pounds of weight. Now, if there are two pounds of weight, and you exert only one pound of power, what becomes of the other pound?"

"It is supported by the fixed end of the line."

"In the purchase-block attached to the mast, we must exert a power equal to one-half of the weight of the mast, the other half being supported by the shears. Bates has made fast the snatch-block in the deck, but we gain nothing in power by its use. What is it for then?"

A dozen hands were raised, but most of the boys were studying the problem. The principal waited until one of these appeared to have made up his mind.

"Without the snatch-block we could only pull on the up-and-down rope, and not more than three or four of us could get hold of it for the want of room to stand near it," replied the student indicated.

"That's the idea exactly," replied the principal.

"Forty of us could get hold of the rope while it is run out from the snatch-block, parallel with the deck," added the thoughtful boy.

"Precisely so; well answered. Then the snatch-block only enables us to change the direction in which the power may be applied. In unloading vessels, they often use a horse to hoist the cargo. The animal could not pull straight down on the rope, but the snatch-block enables him to draw the rope parallel with the top of the wharf. I think you will remember what a snatch-block is, and what it is for. Now man the line."

The students took hold of the line, and walked away with it. The mast rose in the air, and hands were then placed at the guy-lines to keep it in place. When the lower end of the mast was above the deck, Bates took the girt-line attached to the shear-head, and drew the mast into position. Two of the students were sent into the hold to direct the tenon into its step, which is the mortice above the keelson.

The mast was lowered slowly into its place, the square tenon adjusting itself in its place as it belonged, so that there was nothing more to be done, except to wedge it in at the mast-hold in the deck.

CHAPTER XX.

THE SPARS, SAILS, AND RIGGING OF A SHIP.

BEFORE night the two masts of the Lily were in their places, and wedged up so that they would stand alone. After supper there was another lesson in rowing given to the new scholars, and they crossed the lake for the first time.

After the recitations the next day, the students were called to the schoolroom after dinner; and they found on the wall several nautical drawings. The first was a full-rigged ship, "The Queen of the West," a large merchant-vessel. It was drawn in outline, and was so plain that all its parts could be easily seen. The principal stepped upon the platform in front of this drawing, with the pointer in his hand.

"I am going to give you a general idea of the rigging of a ship," said he, when the attention of the school was directed to him. "To obtain all

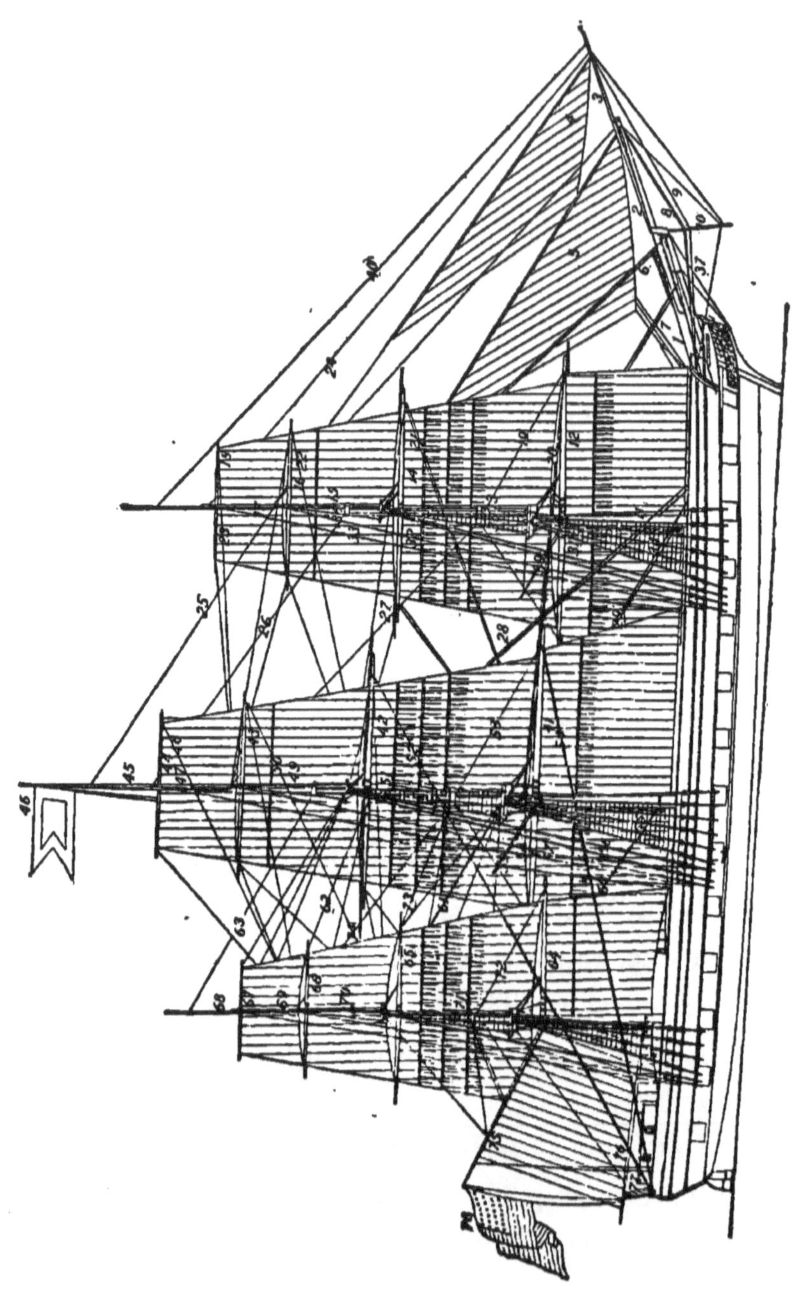

1. Bowsprit.
2. Jib-boom.
3. Flying Jib-boom.
4. Flying Jib.
5. Jib.
6. Fore-topmast-stays.
7. Fore-stays.
8. Jib Martingales.
9. Flying-jib Martingales.
10. Martingale.
11. Foremast.
12. Fore Yard and Sail.
13. Fore-topmast.
14. Fore-topsail Yard and Sail.
15. Fore-topgallant-mast.
16. Fore-topgallant Yard and Sail.
17. Fore-royal-mast.
18. Fore-royal Yard and Sail.
19. Fore-lift.
20. Fore-braces.
21. Fore-topsail-braces.
22. Fore-topgallant-braces.
23. Fore royal-braces.
24. Fore-topgallant-stay.
25. Main-skysail-stay.
26. Main-royal-stay.
27. Main-topgallant-stay.
28. Main-topmast-stays.
29. Main-stays.
30. Fore-spencer-gaff.
31. Fore-topmast-backstays.
32. Fore-topgallant-backstays.
33. Fore-royalmast-backstays.
34. Fore-rigging.
35. Fore-topmast-rigging.
36. Fore-topgallant-rigging.
37. Bobstays.
38. Bowsprit Shrouds.
39. Slings Foreyard.
40. Fore-skysail-stay.
41. Main Yard and Sail.
42. Main-topsail Yard and Sail.
43. Main-topgallant Yard and Sail.
44. Main-royal Yard and Sail.
45. Main-skysail-mast.
46. Burgee, or Private Signal.
47. Main-royal-mast.
48. Main-royal-brace.
49. Main-topgallant-mast.
50. Main-topgallant-brace.
51. Main-topmast.
52. Main-topsail-brace.
53. Main-lifts.
54. Main-brace.
55. Main-rigging.
56. Main-topmast-backstays.
57. Main-topgallant-backstays.
58. Main-royal-backstays.
59. Main-spencer-gaff.
60. Mizzen-stay.
61. Mizen-topmast-stay.
62. Mizzen-topgallant-braces.
63. Mizzen-royal-stay.
64. Mizzen Yard and Sail.
65. Mizzen-topsail Yard and Sail.
66. Mizzen-topgallant Yard and Sail.
67. Mizzen-royal and Sail.
68. Mizzen-skysail-mast.
69. Mizzen-royal-mast.
70. Mizzen-topgallant-mast.
71. Mizzen-topsail.
72. Mizzen-lifts.
73. Mizzen-topsail-braces.
74. Mizzen-topgallant-stay.
75. Spanker-gaff.
76. Spanker-boom.
77. Spanker-sheets.
78. American Ensign.

the details, nothing but practice will suffice. Only a small portion of the rigging of a ship is delineated in this drawing. A sailor has to be so familiar with every part, that he can find any rope in the darkest night, when he cannot see his hand before him.

"You have already learned the names of the three masts, and you can recognize them at a glance. The bowsprit was built into the Lily, and you know it in this ship (1)."

"But there are three sticks in the bowsprit of this ship, when the Lily has only one," suggested Benton Fillwing.

"We could add two more to the Lily if it were advisable. If we added one, it would be the jib-boom (2), which is the middle piece in the picture. The third spar is the flying jib-boom (3). The vertical piece of wood on the end of the bowsprit, through which the jib-boom passes, is called the cap. The stick which points down from the cap (10) is the martingale, or dolphin-striker."

"The sails on the bowsprit are the jibs, are they not?" asked a student who wanted to make a point.

"There are two of them; but we will let the

sails rest until we have disposed of the spars," replied the principal. "Now we will return to the masts. You perceive that there are three of them; but they are not always separate sticks, the two upper ones generally being in one piece. The three lower ones are called simply the masts, and sometimes the lower masts when it is necessary to distinguish them more particularly. The three names I have given you — fore, main, and mizzen — are applied to them, as to all the other masts above them.

"The next mast above is the topmast (13); then comes the topgallant-mast (15); above which is the royal-mast (17). The mast above this is the skysail-mast (45), when there is one. Now I shall point to the different masts, and you will give me the names of them," continued Captain Gildrock, as he placed his pointer on one of them.

"Main-topmast," promptly replied the scholar indicated (51).

The principal moved his pointer.

"Mizzen-royal-mast" (69).

Another was pointed out.

"Fore-topmast" (13).

The principal continued this exercise some time longer, until every student could name any mast of the fifteen in the picture. They were willing, then, to agree with the principal, that the system removed all complications and difficulty; and some of them were quite proud to know so much about a ship.

"There are a few other spars to be remembered," continued the captain, as he fixed his pointer again. "This is the aftermost sail of the ship; and it is called the spanker, though it occupies the place of the mainsail in a schooner or sloop. The stick at the bottom of it is the spanker-boom (76); the one at the top of it is the spanker-gaff (75). There is also a gaff on the mainmast (59), and another on the foremast (30), called spencer-gaffs, with the keywords 'fore' and 'main.'

"At the point where the lower masts join with the topmasts are tops, to the outer edges of which the topmast rigging is set up. At the head of the topmasts are the cross-trees, to which the top-gallant rigging is secured. The round piece of wood at the tip of each royal or skysail mast is the truck, in which holes are made for the passage

of signal halyards, used in hoisting the burgee
or other signal-flags."

The principal proceeded to review the students
by pointing out the spars explained. There was
hardly one of them who made a mistake, for they
had all got hold of the system.

"Now we will examine some of the rigging
of this ship. The same principle is applied to
the ropes as to the spars," continued the principal, pointing to the fore-rigging of the vessel.
"Here are six very large ropes leading from the
top down to the side of the ship. In detail,
these are the shrouds; but the whole is called the
fore-rigging, which may be designated by its side
also, as the starboard or the weather fore-rigging
(34). Across these ropes are drawn smaller
ones, which land-people call rope ladders, but
which sailors call ratlines. But they don't say
they go up the ratlines, any more than that
they go up the rope ladders. They ascend
the fore-rigging. You see a couple of round
things at the lower end of each rope. They are
dead-eyes; each having three holes in it by which
the shroud is hauled taut, or tightened when it
gets loose. Under these are broad pieces of

plank, bolted edgewise to the side of the ship, to sway out the shrouds. The lower dead-eyes are attached to iron bands, running down to the side, and bolted through the timbers, called chains. The planks, or platforms, are channels. The men who sound are sent out on the channels, and are said to stand in the chains.

" The three shrouds extending from the tops to the cross-trees are the topmast rigging, with the keyword before it (35). Above, you have the topgallant rigging. Behind each mast are ropes leading down to the channels, all of which are called backstays, as the fore-topmast-backstay (31), the topgallant-backstay, (32). Of course, these stays may have the name of the side, weather or lee, port or starboard.

" Beginning at the bowsprit, you see a multitude of ropes leading to the foremast, and from one mast to another. These are all called by the general name of stays. The lower one on the bowsprit (7) is the forestay, and leads to the top of the foremast. The next one goes to the fore-topmast-head, and is therefore called the fore-topmast-stay (6). The next two, on which the jibs run, are simply jibstays. From near the end of the flying jib-boom are the fore-top-gallant-stay (24), and the fore-royal-stay, (40).

"The stays between the masts take the names of spars *from* which they lead forward. The mainstay (29) comes from the head of the main-mast. There are a great many of these ropes; but, by observing the rule, you can readily call them by name."

The principal used his pointer for a time, in testing the knowledge of the students; and only through carelessness could they make any mistake.

"Now we come to the sails, but I think you must already know them by applying what you have learned. Only two jibs are set in this drawing, the jib (5) and the flying jib (4). There is one furled, which runs on the fore-top-mast-stay (6), which is the same as the jib in shape, and is called the fore-topmast-staysail. Outside of these three head-sails, — a fourth called the outer jib, and even a fifth the jib o' jib, — these names are differently used.

"The three lower square-sails are called from the names of the mast, the fore, main, and miz-zen sails. Together, they are called the courses;

and sometimes any one of them may be called the fore-course or the main-course, but not often. Formerly, and now among old sailors, the lower yard of the mizzen-mast did not follow the system, but was called the cross-jack-yard, and they pronounced it *crogic*. ˙ No sail was bent to this yard in old times. — Now, what is this?" asked the captain, pointing to the next sail on the fore-mast.

" The fore-topsail " (14).

" This ? "

" The main-topgallant-sail (43)," replied Matt Randolph, clipping the words in sailor fashion.

The captain pointed again.

" The mizzen-royal " (67).

This exercise was continued until the students were entirely at home with the sails. Then the principal pointed to the end of the spanker-gaff.

" This corner of the spanker is called the peak, as it is in any fore-and-aft square-sail. The flag is called the ensign, and the lines by which it is set are the signal halyards. The rope with a block in the middle of it is the weather-spanker vang, the lee-vang is on the other side, and they are used to hold the gaff in place. You observe a rope leading from the mizzen-cross-trees to the spanker-gaff, and from that to the mizzen-mast-head, and back and forth again. This is the spanker-halyards, by which this sail is hoisted. This word applies to all ropes by which sails are hoisted, whether attached to a spar, or to the canvas direct. Now, with what would you hoist the flying jib?"

"With the flying-jib halyards," replied Dick Short.

"When the topsails are set, the yards are hoisted up by halyards. Now, I think we are done with this drawing, and we will take another," continued the principal; and he removed it, and pointed to a new one. "This is a picture of the fore-topsail of a ship, with all the rigging that belongs to it, as well as the two yards by means of which it is set. What is the upper yard called?"

"The fore-topsail-yard," answered Fred Grafton.

"On this yard are the jackstays, which was a rope hauled taut, in old times, and secured to the wood. But in modern times the jackstays are made of wood or iron. However they are made, the sail is secured to the yard by them.

You perceive that the yard is held to the fore-topmast by a band of iron over the mast, so that the cross-spar may slip easily up and down. The halyards are forward of the mast, and pass over a sheave in the head of a topmast. The yard is hoisted by men standing on the deck. The two ropes which run from the mast to the ends of the yard are the lifts by which one end may be raised and the other lowered, which is termed cock-billing the yard. The lines that run down to the middle of the sail are the bunt-lines, and are used to haul up to the yard the bunt, or body, of the sail, when it is clewed up. The double lines that extend from the middle of the yard down to the corners of the sail are the clew-lines, and are employed in hauling up the corners, or clews, of the topsail. The ropes or chains, as may be, which lead from the corners of the topsail to the end of the topsail-yard below are the sheets.

"Nautical language is very exacting on some of these points. For example, we clew up a topsail, but we haul up a course. The clew-lines of a topsail become clew-garnets when applied to a course.

"The blocks at the end of the topsail-yard are for the braces to pass through. These are the ropes by which the yards are set at the proper angle to take the wind. They lead to different parts of the vessel, as convenience requires. At the extreme end of the yard is the jewel-block, through which the halyard of the studding-sail passes. Across the sail are three pieces of canvas, called reef-bands, to strengthen the sail where the reef-points are placed. By the reef-tackle the leech of the sail is drawn up to the yard, and the points tied over the top of the sail. But that will do for to-day."

CHAPTER XXI.

THE RIGGING AND SAILS OF A SCHOONER.

"YOU did not tell us what studding-sails are," said Ash Burton, who had been deeply interested in the explanations given. "You said the halyard of the studding-sail passed through the jewel-block, and that was all."

"I have nothing to illustrate the subject with," replied the principal. "On some of the yards there are extra spars, which can be run out, thus increasing the length of the yard. On these are set the studding-sails. The extra spars are called studding-sail booms"

Captain Gildrock took the chalk, and made a rough drawing of the sails described, so that the pupils could get an idea of them. The students were then dismissed, and after supper pulled the barges over to Sandy Point, where some of them wanted to hear about the removal of Mr. Bristol's cottage from this place to its present location. After the lessons of the forenoon the next day, the work of rigging the boat was continued.

But, before the students went to the wharf, they were assembled in the schoolroom, where a diagram of a schooner was presented to them. The rig was very simple; for she was not to be fitted out as a racing craft, though some of the "kites" used were described.

"The rope, which is sometimes of wire, which passes from the end of the bowsprit to the masthead is the jibstay, which, in our craft, does duty as the forestay. The bobstay leads from the end of the bowsprit on the under side, to the cutwater, to assist in bearing the strain of the jibstay. In a craft of this size it is not necessary to have bowsprit-shrouds and other headgear used in a large vessel. The bobstay is enough.

"We shall put two shrouds on each side of each mast. They have to be set up taut, and they will keep the jibstay tight. The rope passing from the head of the foremast to the head of the mainmast is the spring-stay, which ties the two masts together, and equalizes the strain upon all the rigging."

"A schooner has no tops; but we use a short stick placed across the mast to stay the topmast, sometimes two of them, like the cross-trees of a ship. A single backstay on each side of the topmast is enough to sustain it. From the topmast-head we have a stay, which is the fore-topmast-stay. This is really all the standing-rigging there will be on board the Lily."

"We have not had that term before," suggested Sam Spottwood.

"The two terms 'standing' and 'running' rigging explain themselves," replied the principal. "The former is that which is immovable, except with the vessel: the latter is that by which the sails are set and trimmed, and the various movements of all kinds are effected.

"The other spars of the schooner will be the gaffs and booms, two of each kind, which take their names from the masts to which they are attached. Sometimes there is no boom to the foresail, in which case it is called the lug-foresail. The rope from the mainmast-head to the end of the boom, to support its weight when the sail is not set, is called the topping-lift.

"Now we are ready to look at the sails, and

the rigging necessary to work them," continued the principal, as he pointed to the outlines of the sails on the drawing. "The jib is a three-cornered sail, while the fore and main sails are more nearly square. There are certain names of the parts of the sails which you must learn. The head of the sails is the part attached to the gaffs, while the foot is fastened to the boom. The leach, as a general term, is the outside of the sail. The outer, or after, leach of the mainsail is therefore that part of the sail which reaches from the after end of the gaff to the same part of the boom. The inner leach is next to the mast. This is also called the luff.

"The corners of the sails are called the clews; and you remember that the clewlines of a topsail were to hoist up the corners of the sail. The after corner of the sail at the foot, is also called the tack. On the corners of the courses of a ship, there are ropes for holding the sail in position, which change their names. When the ship is on the wind, the forward one is the tack, and the after one the sheet. When the ship goes about, these ropes change their names, to conform to the general system; which is, that a sheet is the after rope by which the sail is held when full.

"The jib has the same parts as the other sails, though of course it has only three clews; and the same is true of a gaff-topsail. Now, what do you call the line by which we hoist the jib?"

"The jib-halyards," replied Chick Penny, who had got the idea of the system very clearly in his mind.

"The word 'halyards' applies to all sails. What is the rope with which the foresail is hoisted?"

"The fore-halyards," answered Con Bunker.

"And so on. Coming back to the jib, what is the rope attached to the lower corner?"

"The jib-sheet," said Syl Peckman.

"Sometimes, especially in small craft where the sheet leads aft to the standing-room, there are two , of them, which are distinguished as weather and lee jib-sheets. Sometimes the sheet works on a traveller, which is an iron bar extending across the forecastle, on which the ring holding the sheet-block may slip from side to side as the vessel tacks. There must be two flying-jib sheets, so that the sail may be drawn down on each side of the jib-stay, as occasion requires.

"Inside of the hanks or hoops of the jib, where they run on the stay, is a rope leading to the head of the sail, used for hauling it down, and called a downhaul. I have mentioned all the running-rigging of the jibs; though some vessels are provided with additional gear, as the brails, by which the sail is gathered up as it comes down. Now we will pass to the after sails, the jibs taking the general name of head-sails.

"There are two sets of halyards belonging to the fore and main sails. The inner end of the gaff, where it is hollowed out to fit the mast, is called the throat. From this part, the inner halyard gets its name of throat-halyards. They consist of a double purchase, with a rope leading down to the deck on the port side. The peak-halyards are sometimes worked with a double block, and sometimes with several single blocks, fixed at some distance apart on the gaff, so as to divide the pressure. They lead down on the starboard side."

"Which is the larboard-watch?" asked a Vermont boy, who had probably heard the song with this name.

"Larboard and port mean the same thing; but

the former word has gone out of use, because it is so liable to be mistaken for the opposite term, starboard. The two words sounded so nearly alike that mistakes were sometimes made. Some time within a few years, an effort was made in France to adopt the English terms, 'starboard' and 'port,' instead of *stribord*, or *tribord*, as it is now written, and *babord;* though they are not so nearly alike as starboard and larboard."

"Do sailors have to learn the names of terms in foreign languages?" asked Tucker Prince, who seemed to be surprised that the principal knew them.

"Not unless they are to serve in foreign vessels. The Spanish name for starboard is like the French, for it is *estribor;* while port, *babord* in French, is *babor*. In Italian the words are *dritta* and *sinistra*. But if you learn the terms in English, it will be sufficient. The larboard-watch is now called the port-watch. The ship's company are divided into the two watches, called the starboard and port watches.

"Both the fore and the main sail have sheets, each taking the systematic name. Of course, you can all tell where the fore and the main sheet are to be found. Some vessels have brails for gathering up the mainsail when it is lowered, but they are not very common."

"Where is the main-brace?" asked a new student. "I heard a man talking about splicing the main-brace."

"You will not find the main-brace in a schooner, and you will not find the particular one that man meant anywhere, I hope. The main-brace in a ship is one of the two by which the main-yard is is trimmed. Vulgarly, to splice the main-brace, means to take a dram.

"On the mainsail of the Lily, we shall have three rows of reef-points, by which we reduce the sail to as many different sizes as the force of the wind may require. At the outer leach, in line with the reef-points, is a cringle. This is simply a hole, through which a line, called the reef-pendant, is passed, and by which it may be lashed down to the boom. Another is used at the luff; and when the sail is hauled down with the reef-pendants, the points are tied in square knots, so that they can be easily cast loose. In the foresail, we shall have but two reefs; often, there is only one."

"What is a balance-reef?" asked Dick Short, who had never seen any thing of the kind on the lake.

"A row of reef-points is sometimes, but very rarely, extended from the throat of the gaff to the cringle of the upper line of reef-points in the outer leach. When this reef is put in, only the peak of the sail is hoisted. It is used in very heavy weather, when the other reefs are not sufficient.

"On the jib, laced to the lower leach, is a piece of canvas called a bonnet, which makes the jib so much larger. The Lily has a bonnet on her jib, which she will wear except when the wind is so strong as to render it necessary to remove it.

"Through the end of the main gaff is a hole, sometimes fitted with a sheave, through which the ensign-halyards are passed. This is the place to display the American flag, which is the ensign in the navy. On yachts, under certain circumstances, it is carried as a challenge to another yacht to sail with the one carrying it.

"The Lily is to be provided with gaff-topsails, not so much to increase the amount of canvas, as because, among the hills that surround the lake in places, there is often a breeze aloft, when there is none, or next to none, below. These sails are triangular in form, and are usually bent on a pole to which the halyards are attached. Sometimes the sail is shaped like the mainsail, and then the pole becomes a sort of yard. Besides the halyard by which the pole is hoisted, there are two other ropes by which the sail is worked from the deck. The tack passes through a block at the mast-head, so that the inner corner of the sail can be drawn down by it. The sheet, sometimes called the clew, is rigged in a block at the outer end of the gaff, so as to correspond with the other sheets, and passes down to the deck. It is not necessary to go aloft to set the sail, unless something gets foul.

"I have disposed of the ordinary sails of the Lily. She may be provided with several others. On the fore-topmast-stay, we may set a jib-topsail or a balloon-jib. The former is a comparatively small sail; while the latter extends to the topmast-head, and reaches aft to the fore-rigging. It is made of light duck, and is bent to the stay with spring hanks, so that it may be readily taken off and stowed below. This same sail may be used as a spinnaker, in which case, the tack is rigged at the end of a sort of studding-sail-boom carried out from the fore-chains. It is used in either way only when the wind is free; that is, abaft the beam. We might also set a staysail, which is square; the upper clews being hoisted to the topmast-heads, and the tack and sheet secured near the deck. This may be used on the wind."

The students then went to the wharf.

CHAPTER XXII.

ORGANIZING THE SHIP'S COMPANY.

FOR the next week, Bates was the principal instructor of the students on board the Lily while they were employed in putting on the rigging. The short lines which had been on the wharf for a week were in demand, and the old man showed the boys how to make a few of the most useful knots. They were required to repeat the operations till they could make the knots without stopping to dream over them.

The old quartermaster was patient with them while they were attentive to their duty; and in a few days they could make a bowline hitch, tie a square knot, put a clove hitch on a stick, and some others. Then came a lesson in short and long splices, and then in parcelling and serving. Thus trained, the work of setting up the rigging proceeded rapidly; and in a couple of weeks the schooner was rigged and her sails bent.

It was a day of triumph at the school when she was completed, and ready to go forth on the lake. So great was the interest in her, that the Sylph was neglected on Saturdays and holidays. The Lily was large enough to accommodate the entire school of thirty-two ; and immediately after breakfast, on the Saturday after she was finished, all hands were required to be on board of her.

Among the older pupils were two from New-York City, who had received a very fair nautical education on the yacht of the father of one of them. Matt Randolph knew all about a schooner ; for such was the rig of his father's yacht, and he had sailed in her for several years. He had crossed the Atlantic one summer in her, and, from choice, had done duty as a foremast hand. Luke Bennington, his friend, had been with him enough to be very well informed on nautical subjects.

The students were expecting something unusual when they went on board of the schooner that morning. The first thing they were required to do was to tow the Lily out into the middle of Beechwater, which was done with the small boats.

When her anchor went down, Captain Gildrock

opened the business of the day with a speech. As all hands wanted to sail in her, he proposed to organize a ship's company to man her.

"As on board of the Sylph, we shall do every thing by rule," said the principal. "We will divide the ship's company into two watches, and do every thing in nautical style. In the first place we want a captain and two mates. I shall appoint these. For captain, I name Matthew Randolph; for he has had more experience with schooners than any other student."

Not a few of the boys looked at Dory, as though they thought he ought to have been assigned to this position; but he looked serene, and there was no appearance of disappointment visible in his open face.

"For first officer, or mate, I appoint Luke Bennington, who has also had considerable experience in schooners. For second mate, or second officer, Oscar Chester. In merchant vessels, the first officer is called simply the mate. We shall need but two of these officers, one for each watch. Generally, the captain keeps no watch; and, by a certain nautical usage, the second mate is said to keep the captain's watch, which is the starboard."

Oscar Chester, the second mate, wanted to decline the position assigned to him; for he felt that Dory Dornwood, who was considered the most capable student in the school, had been strangely ignored. The principal smilingly declined to permit him to do so. In fact, he had talked this matter over with Dory, who felt that he had received all the honors that belonged to him, and wished to be ignored for the benefit of others.

Captain Gildrock then appointed a cook, who was experienced in his line on board of the steamer, and three stewards. In the forward cabin, there was a cook-stove; and there was a pantry in the cabin, which extended nearly to the foremast.

"I need not say to you, for you have all sailed enough in the Sylph to know it, that all hands must obey their superior officers. Now we will proceed to divide the ship's company into watches. The captain will take the first choice, and the mate the second, and so on until all are stationed."

"Dory Dornwood," said Captain Randolph.

"Thad Glovering," added the mate.

The captain's watch were required to go over to the starboard side, and the mate's to the port side. The principal gave each student a star, with a pin to it, so that it could be stuck on the coat-sleeve. The starboard-watch wore it on the right arm, and the port on the left.

"It is now eight o'clock," said the principal, consulting his watch, and looking at the new captain.

"Quartermaster, strike eight bells," said Randolph, nodding to Dory.

Dory obeyed the order, and struck the required number on a bell, which Mr. Jepson had put up on the bowsprit bitts. He made the sounds by twos, as is the custom on board ship, so that the number may be easily counted.

"The captain has appointed Dory Dornwood and Corny Minkfield quartermasters," said Captain Gildrock. "In the navy, it is the duty of these officers to con the wheel."

"Con the wheel!" exclaimed a student.

"Not a familiar expression on shore, I grant; but that is the word on a naval vessel. It means to watch the wheel, or to oversee the steering," the principal explained. "The sailor who has the trick at the wheel may be careless, and the quartermaster is responsible for the steering. Sometimes two, and even four, men are required to handle the wheel in heavy weather."

The boys were beginning to be impatient; for they were anxious to get under way, to see how the vessel they had built would work, and whether there was any speed in her. But there was not a breath of air stirring, and it would have been useless to hoist the sails. When one asked if they were going to set the sails, the principal explained that it would be worse than folly to do so, for the schooner would certainly drift to the shore, and get aground.

"While we are waiting for a breeze, and we shall soon have one, I will explain something more about the watches," continued the principal. "In getting under way, all hands are on duty, and the first business is to arrange the watches as we have done. The first watch, which is always the starboard, goes on duty at eight on the evening of the first day. It is in charge of the second mate, though the captain may keep it if he chooses.

"This watch serves till twelve o'clock at night; and then the port-watch is called, and the mate takes the deck. At four, the starboard-watch serves the next four hours. The watch from midnight till four in the morning is called the midwatch, that from four in the morning till eight is the morning-watch. From eight till twelve is the forenoon-watch, which comes in at the present time. From twelve till four in the afternoon is the afternoon-watch.

"At this time we come to the dog-watches, which are two hours in length, instead of four, as the others are. Without them the starboard-watch, which was on duty from eight till twelve, and then from four till eight in the morning, would have to take the same place the next night. They were on watch eight hours in the night, while the port-watch served only four.

"During the first dog-watch, from four till six in the afternoon, the port-watch is called. At six, to serve till eight, the starboard-watch has the deck; so that the port will come on at eight, and have eight hours of duty during the second night. The dog-watches therefore equalize the night work. But, in very heavy weather, all hands are liable to be called, and to remain on duty all night.

"When a ship leaves a foreign or domestic port for home, the rule is reversed, and the port-watch goes on duty at eight in the evening. As the sailors say, the captain takes the ship out, and the mate brings her home. But it looks as though we should have a breeze soon, and we are not quite ready for it."

Like the proceedings of a political caucus, every thing seemed to be cut and dried, even to the wind that did not blow; for the principal now produced a bundle of cards, which he called the station-bills. He gave one to each student; and the boy found his own name written upon it, with his duty in all the operations of working the vessel. His place in weighing the anchor, in setting the sails, in coming to anchor, in making a landing at a wharf, and in tacking, were written upon the card.

The principal explained that a short drill was next in order, and directed Captain Randolph to proceed with it. He put the crew through the routine of every manœuvre, and practised it till each student knew his station. The schooner was very heavily manned, and it had required no little skill to divide the work among them. Before the drill was finished, there was quite a ripple on Beech-water, indicating that there was wind enough to give the vessel steerage-way.

"Stations for hoisting the fore and main sails!"

called the captain, at a signal from the principal. There was no nonsense about the work this time, for the schooner was to get under way. The boys were very active, and even Tom Topover moved as though he delighted to obey orders.

Certain hands stationed themselves at the hal-yards, and others stood ready to loose the sails. Orders had been sufficiently established by the drill, to prevent the boys from touching a rope till the command to do so was given.

"Loose sails!" shouted the captain.

"Loose sails," repeated the mate, who was in the waist, and was required to repeat every order when all hands were on duty.

The sail-loosers cast off the stops, which secured the sails to the booms; while a couple of others at each of the masts cast off the halyards, over-hauled them, and saw that they were in order for instant use.

"Hoist fore and main sail!" said the captain; and the order was repeated by the mate, while the second mate was required to see that the work was properly done at the foremast, as the first officer did at the mainmast.

The sails went up as if by magic, so vigorous

were the hands at the halyards. They were swigged up, and the slack taken in, as prescribed in the drill.

"Man the capstan!" called Captain Randolph, when the sails were properly set. "Heave up the anchor to a short stay, Mr. Bennington!"

The mate superintended this operation, and the anchor was soon reported aweigh.

"Man the jib-halyards! Stand by the jib-down-haul!" continued the captain, when the report had been made to him. "The wind is a little south of west, and we will cast on the port-tack."

"On the port-tack, sir," replied the mate, as he went forward to see the order executed.

Enough hands remained at the capstan to trip the anchor; and, as the jib went up the stay, the anchor was lifted from the bottom. Two hands were at the jib-sheets, and, as the sail began to draw, they trimmed it down; and, for the first time in her brief existence, the Lily began to move under sail through the water.

"Three cheers!" shouted Dory Dornwood; and they were given.

CHAPTER XXIII.

THE TRIAL TRIP OF THE LILY.

DORY DORNWOOD had been sent to the wheel; and, as the sails of the schooner filled, he met her with the helm. She heeled over a little, and but a little, for the wind was very light in Beechwater. On the shore, everybody connected with the institution in any capacity had assembled to observe the movements of the new vessel. The three cheers in which Dory had led off drew from them a lively response.

In a few minutes the Lily was near the outlet; but the principal directed the captain to make a turn around the lake, so that all could get a good view of her.

"Ready, about!" shouted the commander to the officers, who repeated the order, and all hands took their stations for tacking.

Dory saw that the Lily had a good full. The

sails fitted extremely well; for they had been made by the firm recommended by Matt Randolph, who had furnished his father's yacht, as well as many others of the highest class.

"Hard a-lee!" continued the captain, when the vessel was in the right place for coming about.

Dory put the helm down, and all the sails shook for a moment; then they began to fill on the other side. As instructed, the hands in charge of the jib-sheets held the sail over till it was filled; and, in this position, it caught the wind sooner than the other sails, and assisted in carrying the head around.

"Draw jib!" said the captain; and the order was repeated by the second mate on the forecastle.

"Slack off the weather-sheet!" added Oscar Chester, who knew his part well, though this was, the first time he had ever sailed in a schooner. "Haul on the lee-sheet! Too much! Ease off a little! That will do; belay the lee-sheet!"

The schooner had come about, and was now standing towards the old wharf, where the people of the institution were assembled, including the ladies from the house and the cottage. The instructors and others cheered lustily, and the ladies waved their handkerchiefs vigorously. Doubtless, the latter wished they were on board; but the principal would not allow any extra persons on board until the ship's company had been well drilled in handling the vessel.

With so many hands, there was very little for them to do; but the captain gave them as much as possible to work off their enthusiasm. He kept those at the sheets tolerable busy hauling in and easing off frequently, to enable him to get the "points" of the craft, as he described it. He let her go free for a moment, and then braced her up to the wind, making all the change he could without tacking.

As the Lily approached the old wharf where the spectators were assembled, he got a course parallel with the shore, and, with the wind a little abaft the beam, allowed her to do her best in a light wind. Her bow was quite sharp, and she was the best model the principal could obtain of the most celebrated modeller in New York. She had been built in strict conformity to the plans and specifications, both in respect to the spars and sails as well as the hull.

It had been unanimously agreed that she ought

to be a fast sailer, by all who had seen her, includ-
some experts who had visited Captain Gildrock.
It remained still to be proved whether or not she
was all that had been hoped and expected of her.
Though she did not wear racing-sails, she was
liberally supplied with canvas. But the wind
in Beechwater was too light to give her a fair
test, and it came in light puffs and squalls.

For the amount of breeze she had, she did
very well; and there was quite a bone in her
teeth as she approached the wharf. The cheers
and signals of the ladies were promptly answered;
for Captain Gildrock was a naval officer of the
old school, and insisted that every compliment
paid to the craft should receive a proper response.
There was no steam-whistle, as on board of the
steamer; and the only way, except with cheers,
to reply, was by dipping the ensign. This was
done several times by Quatermaster Minkfield.

Off the old wharf it was necessary to brace
her up, and she was headed for the mouth of
the creek; but there was no one at the cottage
to salute the new craft, its occupants having
joined the other spectators. The water was deep
at the entrance of the stream; and the captain

ran the schooner a short distance into it, as far as he could and have room to come about.

"Ready, about!" he called to the mate rather sharply, when she had gone as far as he deemed it prudent to proceed up the creek.

She did not tack as handsomely as she had at the other end of the little lake, for the wind was baffling behind the woods on the shore; but she got about with a little humoring. Captain Gildrock smiled, and shook his head, as he looked at Captain Randolph.

"Didn't I do it right, sir?" asked Matt, when he saw that what he had done was not approved, though it was not condemned.

"Perfectly right, so far as handling the schooner is concerned. But you made it possible that we might require the services of the Sylph to assist in getting her off a mud bank," replied the principal, tempering his remark with a smile again.

"I thought I had room enough to go in stays," pleaded the captain of the Lily.

"So you had, so far as the schooner is concerned; but you had to humor her in stays, for the wind was unsteady and puffy.

"Of course it was! What could you expect

in such a place in the woods? There is little wind enough anywhere on Beechwater, but there is less among the trees than in the open water. The principal trouble with boys is that they will run risks. They want to cut a hair off at every corner. They think a young fellow can't be a good boatman unless he takes risks; and, the greater the risk, the better the boatman, in his estimation," continued the principal, in a low tone, so that none of the other students could hear him.

"I didn't think I was taking any risk," added Matt.

"You took the risk of getting aground between two puffs, and nothing but the current of the stream saved you from it," replied Captain Gildrock. "I believe in taking a risk when there is need of it, but never for mere sport, or to show that one is a skilful boatman."

"I am much obliged to you, sir, for speaking to me about it," replied Matt, who did not regard himself as censured; for the principal had a way of condemning an act without hurting the self-respect of the actor.

"I have said it a great many times in school,

and in the various craft, that we should take no
unnecessary risks. I believe that nearly the
whole of the boating accidents result from carelessness. There is no reason why a good boat
should not stay on the top of the water, even in
a gale of wind. If the boat is a good one, — and
it is a risk to go on the water in any other, — she
will float on any sea."

"She may be caught in a squall," suggested
Matt.

"Squalls are always to be expected, and it is
necessary to understand how to deal with them.
At sea, out of sight of land, we have to take
whatever comes. You have sailed a yacht enough
to know what to do in a squall."

"Something may break," suggested Matt.

"Sails and rigging should be frequently over-
hauled, to make it reasonably sure that they will
not give out at a critical moment. It is taking
a needless risk to neglect to do this."

"Then you don't believe that any disasters
ought to occur?"

"I will not go quite so far as that: nine-tenths
of them could be avoided by taking no needless
risk. But we are all human; and while boatmen

will take risks, and be careless, there must be accidents. I advise you to let the pilot take the vessel through the outlet."

Dory Dornwood was the pilot; and he had had more experience in taking sailing craft through the bend of the stream than any other person on board,—or in the town, for that matter. The principal wanted to add, that this same pilot was the most reliable young skipper he had ever known, and for the simple reason that he took no needless risks, though he was ready to incur those which occasion required; but the remark might hurt the feelings of the new captain, and it was not uttered.

The Lily was handed over to Dory, and the ship's company were directed to obey his orders. This was no sacrifice of dignity or authority, for every pilot in charge of a vessel has the absolute command of her for the time. The current of the outlet had piled up banks of sand and mud in places; and it was necessary, in such a comparatively narrow channel, to know where they were.

Dory gave his orders to the mate, and they were executed in the same manner as though they had come from the captain. The wind was better at the V-Point than it had been in the creek, and the pilot had no difficulty in taking the Lily through. She was not as long, by forty feet, as the Sylph; but at one place she had to make a short tack of not much more than twice her length, and it required no little skill to make every thing work so as to avoid a miss-stay.

The schooner came out all right on the river. Captain Randolph resumed the command. The students watched the motion of the Lily with the most intense interest, especially those who had taken a hand in building her hull. The wind freshened as she came nearer to Lake Champlain: she heeled over more, and the bone in her teeth increased in size.

In a little while she passed out of the river into the lake. The wind was now about south-west, and this is always a rather unsteady breeze. As she came to the point at the mouth of the river, the sheets were started, and the schooner went off with the wind on the port-quarter. As the day advanced, the breeze had freshened, till the students had all they wanted. It came over miles of open lake, and there was nothing to obstruct it. The Lily seemed to fly on her course, and the boys were excited to a degree which made them quite noisy. After the sails had been trimmed, there was nothing for them to do except to watch the motion of the vessel.

Captain Gildrock carried his watch in his hand, and had noted the second when the schooner passed the point at the mouth of the river. It was exactly three miles to the headland just beyond the light at Split Rock Point. Dory told his fellow-quartermaster, that the speed of the Lily could not be much less than that of the Sylph when she had a good breeze. She was up with the point ahead before any one had had time to do much thinking over the matter.

"Fifteen minutes from the mouth of the river to Split Rock Point!" exclaimed the principal, looking at his watch.

"Twelve knots an hour!" exclaimed Captain Randolph.

"Not quite," added the principal. "The distances on the lake are given in statute miles. It is only about two and half nautical miles from point to point, and that is only ten knots an hour, which I call very fast sailing."

The principal gave the speed to the rest of the

students, and then explained the difference between nautical and statute miles.

"The Lily will do better than that yet," said Captain Randolph, "for we have not hurried her; and, with the gaff-topsails, I think she will be good for twelve knots an hour."

The principal assented to the proposition.

CHAPTER XXIV.

A LIVELY BREEZE ON LAKE CHAMPLAIN.

THE trial trip of the Lily was certainly a success so far, but her captain was not quite satisfied. She had made ten knots an hour; and he wanted to know if she was not equal to twelve, which was the ordinary speed of the Sylph. Above Split Rock the lake begins to widen, and the schooner had plenty of searoom. The sea had become tolerably smart, and the Lily pitched in a very oceanic style. The boys liked this sort of thing, though some of the new hands began to be seasick.

At the request of Captain Randolph, the principal consented to the setting of the gaff-topsails. It was blowing very fresh now; and it was not a very easy thing to get these sails aloft, especially with a crew not a half a dozen of whom had ever seen a gaff-topsail set. Even Dory had never seen this sail set, except at a distance; but he was perfectly familiar with the theory.

The lake was now covered with white caps, and the sea seemed to be increasing. The principal was rather sorry that he had consented to the setting of the gaff-topsails. He was the only adult on board, for even Bates had been left on shore. He finally modified his consent, after the sails had been brought up from below, so as to require that the Lily should be anchored under the lee of Cannon's Point when the gaff-topsails were set.

The captain gave the order to brace her up, and run for the point indicated. The crew were astonished when the order came for them to take their stations to anchor the schooner. When she luffed up, the jib was hauled down; and, at the right time, the anchor was let go.

"Stations for setting the gaff-topsails!" called the mate, who had received the order for the work from the captain.

By this time the boys had studied their station-bills enough to know their duty, and they had been drilled in doing it. While waiting for a breeze, they had set both gaff-topsails at the same time; and off Cannon's Point it was done as well as it had been in the quiet of Beechwater.

"Stations for weighing anchor!" called the captain.

The students were happy again, and even happier than before; for the extra sails had been set, and they were to be under way again. In a few minutes more — for, with so many hands, very quick work was made of all the manœuvres, — the Lily was standing down the lake again. The gaff-topsails made a wonderful difference in the action of the schooner, for they took the wind from above the bluffs.

With the wind on the port-quarter, the schooner seemed to leap like a greyhound on her course. It was evident that she was an able sea-boat; for she lifted handsomely on the waves, and did not bury her bows in the water. She carried a strong weather-helm; though the power gained by the horizontal wheel made it easy to steer her, much easier than it would have been even with a long tiller.

Captain Gildrock measured the distance from Cannon's Point to Burlington, where he had directed the captain to put in, and found it was six miles to a certain spot near the breakwater. He was sorry he had forgotten to bring a log-line with him. He took the time of the departure, after the schooner was fairly under way.

"I shall ask you for a boat off Burlington when you get under the lee of the breakwater, for I have to go to the bank," said the principal to the captain. "I shall be busy there for two hours; and, while I am on shore, you may run over to Au Sable Point, which is about far enough to use up the time. Do you think you can get along without me?"

"I should be glad to have you with us all the time; but I am sure I can handle the schooner, for I have navigated the Sea Sprite for a whole day in the absence of the sailing-master," replied Captain Randolph confidently.

"The wind is blowing rather fresh, but the Lily proves herself to be an able sea-boat. The only thing to fear is, that some of your crew may give you trouble."

"I don't think they will be likely to do so on the first trip; but, if any do, I think we can manage them, for I am sure all the old scholars will stick by me."

"I don't believe you will have any trouble, and you will be likely to be back in less than two hours. I will get through as soon as I can."

There was nothing about the crew that indicated a mutiny, or even any trouble; for all of them obeyed orders with the nicest care. It was a new thing; and the boys were not likely to make trouble, if ever, until the schooner had become an old story. Hardly any of them had ever seen any livelier sailing on the lake, and half of them had hardly ever been in a sailboat. Half a dozen of them were too seasick to hold up their heads. Among them was Pell Sankland, and even Kidd Digfield was able only with a struggle to keep his place in the ranks.

The government charts of Lake Champlain have a scale on each sheet, in statute miles, nautical miles, and kilometres. The principal had taken off the distance to the point in Burlington Harbor, from the scale of sea-miles. In exactly thirty minutes from the departure from Cannon's Point, the Lily was abreast of the mark; and the distance was six knots. The yacht had therefore made her twelve knots an hour; and the fact was announced to the ship's company, whereat they gave three rousing cheers.

As he had been directed to do, the captain ran the schooner behind the breakwater. The order had been given for the port-quarter boat to be made ready, and her crew of five were called away. The hands had learned how to lower a boat, on board of the steamer; and the work was done properly, and to the admiration of a crowd of spectators on the steamboat wharf, who had run to see the new craft.

The principal was landed, and the boat returned. The captain ordered it to be hoisted up at the davits; though Tom Topover, who was one of the crew, grumbled. It would have to be lowered again in a few minutes, and what was the use of hoisting it up, he reasoned.

But he was hardly on deck before the order was given to get up the anchor; and the Lily was soon standing to the northward, inside of the break-water. At the lower beacon, she hauled in her sheets, and a course to the north-north-west was given out. The sea was breaking over the top of the breakwater, and outside of it the lake was decidedly rough. At this point the lake is twelve miles wide, so that there was room enough to stir up big waves for an inland sheet of water.

"We are going off without Captain Gildrock," said Tom Topover, after the sheets had been properly coiled up.

"Why shouldn't we?" asked Nim Splugger, to whom the remark had been addressed; for he was the only one of the remaining original Topovers who could hold his head up, Kidd Digfield having just succumbed to the malady, after holding out as long as he could.

Nearly one-half of the ship's company were seasick, and Captain Randolph had begun to fear that he might be short-handed before he returned to Burlington. Even some of the old students were sick.

"I think I could manage this thing as well as Matt Randolph," continued Tom Topover, looking into Nim's face with interest. "I know all about sailing a boat now. I have been out twice with Dory in the Goldwing, and he showed me how to steer her."

"I think I should rather have Matt than you in command," added Nim. "I can steer, but I shouldn't want to have to manage a boat of this size."

"I should like the fun of it; and, if our fellows

were as good as they used to be, I would get hold of her, and have a cruise on our own hook," said Tom. (And it appeared that he had lost none of his former enterprise, however it might be with his late cronies.) "But they have all joined the church, and there is no more fun ahead for us."

"Joined the church!" exclaimed Nim.

"I mean old Gildrock's church. They are all as proper as lambs; and the fun has all gone out of them, you among the others, Nim Splugger."

"I think there is as much fun in me as there ever was," added Nim.

"Why don't you show your colors then? You are as meek as Moses."

"So are you!"

"I couldn't do any thing all alone. The fellows caved in, and did not take any more notice of me than they did of any other fellow," growled Tom, who evidently believed that he was born to be a great leader among men.

"It was no use for a fellow to bite his own nose off," Nim explained, as he and the others had done twenty times before to Tom, who had always been ready to remove his nasal appendage in the manner indicated. " If you want to do any thing that is reasonable, just let the fellows know, and you will see where they stand. They have not joined Captain Gildrock's church any more than you have."

" I. have had a pretty good time since I was raked into the Industrial School, and I have not thought much about studying up any thing in the way of fun; but it is getting to be a little heavy on my hands to be tied to a bell-rope, and keep step with some little lamb like Dory Dornwood."

The conversation was interrupted just as Tom Topover had delivered himself of these sentiments. The first officer had discovered that all the hands stationed at the jib-sheets were seasick, which was a very humiliating state of things to the captain, and some changes had become necessary in the station-bills. Four hands were transferred from the fore and main sheets to the jib.

The Lily had the wind on the beam; and there was nothing to be done, till the order, " Ready, about!" was given off Point Au Sable. The schooner came about in the liveliest manner, and stood for Burlington on the opposite tack. She was soon inside of the breakwater, and came to anchor there. The other quarter-boat was sent to the shore; and, after waiting a short time, it brought off the principal.

The deck had the appearance of a hospital-ship when the principal came on board, and he directed the captain to beat up Shelburne Bay. Under the lee of the point, where the water was smooth, the Lily came to anchor, to give the seasick ones a rest. The cook and stewards had been at work getting dinner, and at twelve it was served in the cabin. But not many more than half of the students wanted any dinner, and some of them said they did not want any more sailing on the lake.

The dinner was creditable to the cook, and was heartily enjoyed under the novel circumstances. The seasick ones rapidly recovered, and soon wanted something to eat. But the sea continued heavy all the rest of the day, and the principal changed his plan; for he had intended to make a trip to Isle La Motte, and return after dark, in order to give the students a practical exemplification of the use of the signal-lights, as well as of navigating by course and compass. It happened that this had to be deferred till the following week; for an event occurred at the school, a little later, which caused the principal some trouble.

The Lily returned to her moorings early in the afternoon.

CHAPTER XXV.

TOM TOPOVER IN THE ASCENDANT AGAIN.

THE Lily was to make another excursion on the following Saturday; and Marian Dornwood and Lily Bristol were to be passengers, as well as their mothers. The principal had predicted the strong breeze which had prevailed during the first trip, but it was just what was desired for a trial trip. The schooner had proved herself to be a very able sea-boat, and had exceeded all expectations in regard to her speed. She was easily managed, and "filled the bill" in every respect.

She was entirely finished now; and, on the following Monday, all hands went to work in the shops again, in the afternoon. Some of the new scholars, who had shown more taste for work in iron and brass than in wood, were set to work with a file; for this was the first lesson given to the machinist. Among these was Tom Topover; and it was found, in a few days, that, after some experience, he was the best filer of the new-comers. His eye proved to be good, and the principal was much encouraged in regard to him.

Since the first vain efforts to get up a rebellion, he had behaved very well; and as he was not allowed to go beyond his depth, either in the schoolroom or the shop, he had appeared to be quite satisfied with his condition. Mr. Bentnick insisted that he was reformed and entirely reconstructed. Mr. Brookbine was of the same mind. But Captain Gildrock shook his head, and did not believe it, though he saw that the fellow was wonderfully improved.

"He gives us no trouble at all," said Mr. Jepson; "and he handles a file better than any new boy I have had."

"Intellectually, he is not much of a scholar, and he never will be brilliant in his studies; but he learns his lessons a good deal better than some of the brighter boys," added Mr. Bentnick; "I have great hopes of him."

"So have I," added the principal: "but he is one of the students who is almost sure to make a slip sooner or later, and it will not surprise me at any time, to find him getting up a conspiracy. The trouble is, that he has no high aim, — in fact, no aim at all. He is not yet trying to be any thing or any body. He is doing very well just now, simply because he is interested. He learns his lessons because he don't like to be a prisoner in his room. It will take but a little thing to throw him off his balance."

"I think he wants to be a machinist, and I reckon he has a fancy for running an engine," said Mr. Jepson.

"If you believe it, encourage him by all means. The first thing to be accomplished in his case, is to plant some kind of an ambition in his being. If he wants to be an engineer, the desire is capable of making a decent man of him; though I am afraid he will always be, to a greater or less degree, uncertain and unreliable."

Hardly a week passed without the appearance at the school of one or more visitors, for it was a rather novel institution. It had been written up in the newspapers, and been the subject of a discussion in an educational meeting. About the middle of the week after the trial trip of the Lily, half a dozen gentlemen came to Beech Hill, in the afternoon, but not particularly to see the workings of the institution. They were capitalists who desired to interest Captain Gildrock in an enterprise in which they were engaged. But when they got there, they were invited to inspect the workshops, and look over the grounds. They were pulled off to the Lily, which was exhibited as a specimen of the workmanship of the students.

They had been so much interested in what they saw, and so much absorbed in the business that had brought them to Beech Hill, that they remained till the supper-bell rang. They were invited to remain to tea, and accepted the invitation. Afterwards they went out to Beechwater to see the students in the barges, who still practised with the oars every evening. By this time the rowing was almost perfect, even among the new pupils.

It was getting dark when the crew of the Winooski came from the boat-house. In the walk, Tom Topover was observed to pick up something; but, as he did not say he had found any thing, no further notice was taken of the fact. He went to the dormitory with the others, and a keen observer might have seen that he was a good deal elated about something. But Tom was as cunning now as he had ever been, though that is not saying much. It was a low cunning, and Tom believed he was at least ten times as smart as anybody considered him to be.

Kidd Digfield and Pell Sankland went to work upon their examples in arithmetic, which related to a practical subject; and they were interested in them. While they were at work, Tom and Nim Splugger paid them a visit. Although the bond which bound them together was not as strong as it had been, it still existed; and they associated more with each other than with the other students, though they were quite intimate with Bent Fillwing and Jack Dumper, who were regarded as two of the hardest characters among the recruits.

"I am spoiling for a good time," said Tom Topover, as he seated himself on the bed in Kidd's room.

" What kind of a time are you spoiling for? — such a one as we had last Saturday?" asked Kidd, who had been so seasick, that he did not remember the trial trip with much satisfaction.

"I didn't get seasick, and I had a good time," replied Tom. "But the thing was a little too stiff for me. There was too much officer about the whole thing to suit me. But I should like to take a trip in the Lily, and have it on our own hook."

"Do you believe you could handle her?" asked Pell.

"I know I could. I have learned to steer, for I had one trick at the wheel, and I have stood at the helm on board of the Sylph."

"But the steering is only a small part of handling a boat," suggested Kidd. "A fellow has to know what is under water as well as above it."

"I could take that schooner up to Rouse's Point — and that is as far as I ever went — as well as Captain Randolph," persisted Tom, with a good deal more spring in his manner than he had displayed of late.

"I don't know but you could," added Kidd, turning to his slate.

"There isn't any fun in you, Kidd Digfield, since you got into this school. I believe you like it as well as Ash Burton and Sam Spottwood," added Tom, with no little disgust in his manner. "I tell you I am spoiling for a time, such a time as we used to have."

"What sort of a time?" asked Kidd, looking up at him.

"A regular out-and-out bender," chuckled Tom, showing more of his mysterious spring than before.

"I don't know what you want yet," replied Kidd. "Do you mean to get into some scrape?"

"I don't believe that if I got three miles from this concern, I should ever get back again," added Tom significantly.

"Do you want to run away?" asked Kidd, dropping his voice.

"That's about the color of it," answered the ex-chief, with a wink.

"I don't think I want to get away," replied Kidd, turning to his slate again.

"I don't say I shall run away, but I do say I am going on a time," continued Tom, in a whisper, as though the walls might have ears. "I must have some fun, even if I have to spend a week in the brig for it."

"What kind of a time? Why don't you say what you mean, and not beat about the bush all night," demanded Kidd, who was certainly filled with curiosity, even if the memory of past exploits with the Topovers did not influence him.

"And you will go to old Gildrock, and tell him all about it!" exclaimed Tom.

"That's too bad, Tom!" said Kidd, springing to his feet in his excitement. "Did you ever know me to do such a thing?"

"I never did; but you have become a little lamb, and the shepherd leads you with a silk thread. There is no knowing what you will do," muttered Tom.

"You ought to know that I won't do a mean thing," returned Kidd indignantly. "I don't believe in bucking against a stone wall as you do, but I am no more of a lamb than you are."

Kidd certainly was not very thoroughly reformed, or he would not have so indignantly repelled the charge of being a good boy. To be able to bear such scoffs and taunts was the next lesson he had to learn, and it was a great pity that he had not learned it sooner. But he could not bear to be reproached because he had behaved himself. This is the misfortune of any boy who has earned a bad reputation, — that he feels obliged to sustain his bad name.

"You never used to do mean things, but since you became a little lamb" —

"I am not a little lamb!" protested Kidd, more angry than he would have been if he had been called a thief. "I mean to get along as easy as I can, and I don't care about living on bread and butter and cold water. This is a free country, and every fellow that wants to do so can put his fingers into the fire."

"Do you want to have a little fun, Kidd Digfield? That's the question before the house just now, as the nobs say," continued Tom Top-over, dropping his voice down to a confidential tone.

"It depends upon what sort of fun it is," replied Kidd. "If you mean the fun of being locked into your room for a week, and be fed on short rations, I don't want any fun."

"I don't mean that, or any thing of that kind," said the ex-chief," going to the door, and looking out into the hall to see if any listeners were near. "I mean some real out-and-out fun, like a sail by ourselves, a day or two at a hotel, spending the nights at the theatre, or some such place."

"I shouldn't object to something of that sort," replied Kidd; and Pell Sankland began to look as though he felt an interest in the subject of the conversation, for he put his slate on the table, and gave his attention to the conversation.

"Now you begin to act like yourself," added Tom approvingly.

"But what's the use of talking about such a time?" Kidd objected.

"It takes money, and a lot of it, to go to a hotel and the theatre. Besides, there are no theatres within twenty miles of Beech Hill."

"There is one in Burlington, another in Plattsburgh," returned Tom. "As to money, there will be enough of that."

"Enough of that? Do you mean that you have got any money?" demanded Kidd.

"I don't mean to say any thing about it," added the ex-chief, who seemed to be regaining his old sway over his companions. "All I've got to say is, that if you want to have some fun of the sort I have spoken of, just say the word, and don't ask any questions."

Kidd raised some objections, and so did Pell; but Nim Splugger appeared to have been taken into the confidence of the Topover in the beginning, for he treated all that was said as a matter of course. Tom called Kidd and Pell "little lambs " a few times; and this seemed to have more effect than any other arguments, albeit it was no argument at all. Kidd and Pell did not want to yield, but they were driven into submission by the raillery of Tom and Nim. At nine o'clock they had crept out of the dormitory, and found Bent Fillwing and Jack Dumper at the old wharf.

CHAPTER XXVI.

AN INDEPENDENT LEADER.

SINCE the Topovers and the other hard boys had behaved themselves so well, all precautions were relaxed; for the principal knew that barred windows were a standing temptation for them to escape. The students were allowed all the liberty it was practicable to give them. The bars had been removed from the windows of the restless spirits, as soon as they showed a spirit of subordination.

All the students retired at whatever time they pleased, provided that it was before ten o'clock. All lights were to be put out at that hour, and one of the instructors always passed through the halls of the dormitory at this time. The boys were required to lock their doors; and, when it was found that the door was locked and the light put out, that was sufficient evidence that the occupant of the room had gone to bed.

Tom Topover had instructed his gang to lock their doors, and put the keys in their pockets. If they succeeded in reaching the old wharf, which was the place appointed, without being seen, they would be safe. They passed out of the dormitory one at a time, and crept very cautiously to the meeting-place.

It was evident that Tom had opened the subject to Bent Fillwing and Jack Dumper before he said any thing to his former comrades. But he was careful not to say a word of the details of his plan to any one. He had caught this idea from the principal, and the officers of the steamer. They never said what they were going to do, and always insisted on blind obedience. He had followed their example, as well for the sake of prudence as in order to preserve his power over his companions. He believed in "sealed orders," and he kept his own counsel.

Nim Splugger had entered readily into the spirit of the enterprise, whatever it might prove to be; but Kidd and Pell were sorry a dozen times before they reached the old wharf. They would have turned back, if they had learned to bear the ridicule of Tom and Nim.

"Now what is all this about, Tom?" asked Bent Fillwing, who had been the terror of the town in which he lived before he came to Beech Hill.

"You will find out all about it in due time," replied Tom.

"But I want to to find out now," Bent insisted.

"I can't tell you a thing now. All you have to do is to obey orders," replied Tom serenely, as though he believed it was all right,

"Obey orders? Whose orders?" asked Bent, with an obvious sneer.

"Mine, of course. I got this thing up; and I am going to see it through, whatever it costs."

"Oh, you are!" snuffed Bent. "But I prefer to know something more about it before I go any farther."

"Not a thing!" exclaimed Tom. "If you don't want to join, you can go back to your room and study your lessons. I have had lessons enough for a while, and I don't believe old Gildrock will see me again very soon. I am a free man!" blustered Tom.

"Do you expect us to follow your lead without

knowing where we are going, or what we are to do?" demanded Bent, rather sharply.

"I have said enough to let you know that we are to take a sail, that we are going to a hotel, and that we shall go to the theatre or the circus, if we can find one. I saw some big bills, with colored pictures, on the fences near the wharf in Burlington; and I guess there is a circus somewhere in these parts."

"That's all very well, but we don't know that you can do all you say you can," replied Bent, moved by the bill of fare which their leader held out to them.

"I can do all that, and a great deal more," answered Tom, chuckling, and with an air of confidence which seemed to have its influence upon his companions.

"It takes money to go to a hotel, or to get into a theatre or a circus," continued Bent; and not one of the party had ever been any nearer to an equestrian performance than the outside of the canvas.

"I know that as well as you do," replied Tom, as he put one of his hands into his trousers-pocket, as if to emphasize his remark.

"If you have got any money, say so, and tell us how much you have," said Jack Dumper. "What's the use of being so secret? It don't do any good."

"Do you suppose I am going to have any one of you fellows that gets mad, running back to old Gildrock, and telling him what I have got in my trousers-pocket, where we are going, and what we are going to do? Not if I know myself. And Tom Topover thinks he knows himself better than any other fellow knows him. That's the whole of it. I won't trust you any farther than I have said; and you can all go back if you like, and I will carry out the plan myself, without any help from any of you. I can get along well enough alone, and I know where to go and what to do."

This independence was too much for the rest of them ; and, though Bent growled, he submitted. They were all sure by this time that the chief had plenty of money, and they wondered with all their might where he had obtained it. There was no report of any theft about Beech Hill, and most of the boys never left the grounds except in the boats.

"I don't like this way of doing it, but I hate

to back out," said Bent, when Tom had delivered himself, in full, of his opinions and intentions. "The fairest thing would be to tell what you are going to do, Tom; and then the fellows can't find any fault if things go wrong."

"The fellows may find fault if they like: what do I care for that? If I find the money and the brains for the scrape, I ought to have the management of the thing."

"Nobody objects to your managing it," said Jack Dumper. "But we should like to know what you are going to do."

"You won't know from me," replied Tom doggedly. "If any fellow wants to back out, now is the time for him to make tracks."

Kidd and Pell were tempted to accept the invitation.

"I don't want any little lambs with me," added Tom; and this remark upset the two penitents, and they had not the pluck to retire from the enterprise.

Tom Topover continued to talk for some time longer in a low tone, so that no one who happened to be out could hear him. He was waiting for the timid ones to withdraw, but no one did so.

The good time promised influenced Bent and Jack, while the fear of ridicule upset the good intentions of Kidd and Pell. It was evident enough that Tom intended to take one of the boats; and it must be one of the sailboats, for all the barges and rowboats were locked up in the boathouse.

But at the old wharf there was a skiff, which was used when the Goldwing was to be brought in for a party. It was not large enough to accommodate more than three with safety, and Tom divided his forces for the trip. It was not till after ten that he did this, and the lights were all put out in the dormitory. Even the mansion was shrouded in darkness; for all the people in it were early risers, and had retired before this time. It was clear that the absent ones had not been missed at the dormitory.

Tom sent Nim back for the three who had been left on shore; for he would not trust either Kidd or Pell, lest they should back out and give the alarm. He could control them while they were in his presence, but he was afraid of them if they were out of sight. The messenger could bring only two of them, and he went a second time for

the last one, who happened to be Bent Fillwing.
To the surprise of this worthy, he found that the
leader had taken possession of the Lily, instead
of the Goldwing, which he supposed would be the
one selected. He objected with all his might to
the selection.

"This is the stupidest thing you ever did in
your life, Tom Topover!" he exclaimed, when he
met the commander of the expedition on the
forward deck of the schooner.

"What is?" asked Tom coolly.

"To take the Lily when there are only six of
us," repeated Bent, rounding up fully the expression of his wonder at the folly of the leader.
"What are you going to do in this big boat?"

"The fun of sailing her is half what the trip
is for," added Tom. "If you don't want to go in
the Lily, there is the skiff, and you know the way
to the shore. I don't want you, if you won't take
things as they come and quit grumbling. I am
going to do all the grumbling myself."

"You always do it all, and it is not fair to give
the other fellows no chance at all," replied Bent,
struggling to be as facetious as the chief. "It
took thirty-two of us to handle her last Saturday;

and six of us have no show, and in the night too.
How are you going to get through the outlet with
her? You are no pilot, and Dory Dornwood is
fast asleep by this time.'

"I can take her through as well as Dory. I
don't want any more growling. If you are not
satisfied, Bent, go ashore, wrap yourselves up in
your wool and go to sleep. I am the captain of
this ship."

"Perhaps you are!"

"I know I am. Did you hear any fellow growling to Matt Randolph last Saturday?"

"He had the principal behind him. Besides,
some of the fellows will get seasick, and then who
will handle this big schooner. I move you put it
to vote, whether we go in the Goldwing or the
Lily," continued Bent, suddenly assuming a pleasant tone.

"I don't care how you vote, or what you want
to do. I am going in the Lily, and any fellow
who don't want to go with me can go on shore,
and go to bed," said Tom decisively.

That settled the question. Tom did not hear
the remarks the principal made to the captain of
the schooner, in regard to taking risks; but he de-

termined to run no needless risk on the present occasion. Though everybody appeared to be asleep at Beech Hill, Captain Gildrock might be wandering about the estate; for he was a man who was very likely to turn up unexpectedly when any mischief was in progress. Tom waited till he heard the town-clocks strike eleven. It was safe then, in his opinion, to proceed.

The leader of the Topovers had certainly learned a great deal since he had been a pupil at Beech Hill. The principal, to encourage him when he appeared to be doing well, had humored him a good deal. He had steered the steamer and the Goldwing, and could handle a sailboat about as well as the average boy who did not pretend to be a boatman.

The moorings of the Lily were so near the dormitory and the stables, that Tom was afraid to hoist the fore and main sail of the schooner, lest any noise should be heard on shore. The old quartermaster had a room over the carriage-house, and he slept with one eye open. The moorings were cast off into the skiff, and the Lily was allowed to float on the current. It took her a long time to get to the outlet. With all his boasted skill, Tom was afraid to sail the schooner through the outlet in the darkness.

He rigged a pair of large oars in the fore-rigging, and put his crew on the handles. They obtained headway enough to give her steerage-way, and the pilot had no trouble in keeping the Lily in the middle of the stream. With no little difficulty, and a great deal of jaw, the sails were set, and the schooner stood down the river.

The wind was light; but in half an hour she passed into the lake, and Tom headed her to the north.

CHAPTER XXVII.

A SLEEPY SHIP'S COMPANY.

THE wind was from the west, and there was but little of it. Tom knew a great deal more about sailing a boat than when he tried to handle the Goldwing; and he trimmed the sails on the port-tack so that the schooner went along very well, though she was making not more than two knots an hour. It was very dark, and the gloom of the night was rather trying to the new skipper. But he could see the light on Split Rock Point, and steered for that.

It was very quiet on the lake at midnight, for there was nothing to create a particle of excitement. There was nothing to be done to the sails; for Tom could hardly see them, and he was not skilful enough to know their condition from the feeling. He had sent Kidd Digfield and Pell Sankland to the forecastle to keep a lookout, while the other four remained in the standing-room with the chief.

Tom had hardly laid a course before his companions began to gape and yawn. Not one of them was accustomed to being up at so late an hour; and all of them had done a day's work in the shop, and pulled the Winooski for an hour after supper. They were tired; and, when the first excitement of Tom's scheme had died out, they began to wish they were in bed in their rooms.

The lookout on the forecastle were troubled in the same way. There was nothing to do, and little to think about. The leader's sealed orders did not permit any play of the imagination; and what the day would bring forth they could not imagine, even if every thing worked as Tom expected. Kidd gaped, and Pell gaped. They found the softest places on deck, and stretched themselves out. In a few minutes they were both fast asleep.

With the wheel in his hands, Tom had enough to keep him awake for a time. Bent Fillwing had not a great deal of confidence in the seamanship of the skipper, and he kept watch of the course of the boat. But, with the light ahead, it was not easy for him to go wrong; for there were no islands or dangerous places in the course.

"Are we all to sit up all night, Tom?" asked Bent, when he had nearly dislocated his jaws with gaping. "Some of us might as well go to bed, and sleep till morning."

"I guess not," replied Tom. "Do you want to leave me alone on deck?"

"Why can't we have watches, just as we had on the trial trip?" asked Bent, gaping again.

"All right. In that case we shall want a mate, and I appoint Nim Splugger. I will keep the other watch myself."

If Bent had not been rather more than half asleep, he might have rebelled at this selection; for Nim was generally regarded as one of the poorest sailors in the crew. But he made no objection; though Nim, conscious of his lack of ability, declined the position. He did not feel competent to take charge of the vessel in the absence of the skipper. He whispered his thought to Tom, and suggested that he should appoint Bent to the position.

"I won't do it!" exclaimed Tom decidedly.

"Won't do what?" demanded Bent, who heard

this answer, though he had not heard Nim's sug·
gestion.

The skipper made no reply, but he insisted that
Nim would do very well, and must be mate,
whether he were willing or not. Bent Fillwing
had a mind of his own, and he was disposed to
resist the authority of the leader sometimes. Tom
was afraid to make him his second in command.
He feared that Kidd and Pell might be weak
when he needed their support, and he could not
depend upon them. Jack Dumper was about the
same sort of a cipher as Nim.

"If Nim is to be mate, let us have the crew
divided into watches," said Bent impatiently, and
with a succession of yawns.

"I choose Jack Dumper," added Tom.

"I take Bent Fillwing," continued Nim, sub-·,
mitting to the greatness thrust upon him.

"Pell Sankland," said the captain.

"Kidd Diggfield," followed the mate, taking
the last.

"According to rule, the captain's watch has the
deck, and the port-watch can turn in," continued
Bent, rising from his seat. "We are to sleep for
the next four hours. You will call us at four in
the morning, Tom."

"I shall call you when I want you," said Tom sharply; for Bent talked as though he were the skipper, and he damaged the dignity of the captain.

"By that time you can hear the church-clocks at Burlington, and you will know when it is four o'clock. Now, Nim, go forward, and call Kidd Digfield.

"Go yourself, Bent," interposed Tom, who thought the speaker was giving off orders as though he thought he was the captain.

But Nim was not injured by the words of his subordinate, and he went forward. He roused the sleepers, and informed them that they were divided into watches, and Kidd could turn in. He was glad enough to do so, and he followed the mate to the cabin. This apartment was a good-sized room, and contained four berths. They were all furnished; and every thing on board was in place, as though she had been prepared for a long voyage. There was a lantern hanging to a beam, which Bent lighted. Without a moment's delay they turned in, and were soon asleep.

Pell Sankland wished he had been in the star-board-watch, but it was all the same to him. He turned over and went to sleep again, as soon as Kidd had gone below. Jack Dumper had reclined on the cushioned seats of the standing-room, and he was asleep almost as soon as the lookout on the forecastle.

Tom Topover had an imagination, coarse and low as it was; and its wings were not clipped by the secrecy which limited the thoughts of his companions. The Lily passed Split Rock Light, and the lake was wider than below this point. The wind freshened a little, and the schooner increased her speed.

Tom did not feel quite as much at home as he had before. The gloom of the night vexed him, and the water looked black. He had never been a close observer of the lake; but he knew that there were islands between the mouth of Beaver River and Burlington, and it would not be a difficult matter to run over them. He had never sailed at night before, and knew nothing of the position of the lights, except the one on Split Rock Point. He could see another ahead, just as far as he could see at all; but he had forgotten where it was, if he had ever known.

The skipper was troubled, and spoke to Jack

Dumper; but the fellow was fast asleep. He stood up, and looked ahead to see if there were any obstructions in his course. He could see nothing, but he lacked confidence. He thought of calling Bent, for he knew more about the lake than any other fellow on board; but he could not ask for help from one who aspired to power. In spite of himself and the perplexity of his position, he began to gape and yawn. He was so sleepy he could hardly keep his eyes open, and something must be done.

Taking Jack Dumper by the collar, he dragged him off the cushions before he could get a word out of him. His watch-mate knew less than the skipper about the lake. He could not tell any thing about the islands. He sent him forward to ask Pell. The lookout was roused with difficulty; and, when he was awake, he was so heavy that he could not remember that there was a single island in the lake. Tom rated both of his watch-mates for going to sleep; and, putting the helm down, he directed them to haul in the sheets. They knew how to do this, and it was done.

The skipper could keep his eyes open no longer,

and he dropped asleep once at the wheel. But the shaking of the sails waked him in a minute. He had headed the Lily for Cannon's Point, where she had anchored on Saturday. He called on his watch to haul down the jib and let go the anchor. The wind was light, and he did not lower the other sails. He dismissed the watch, and they all went below. Tom took the remaining berth, and his two companions laid down on a divan. They were asleep as soon as they had stretched themselves out.

When the sun rose, it brought up a breeze with it from the south-west. The sails which had been left in a very unseamanlike condition, began to rattle and bang. They filled, and the schooner forged ahead until she was brought up by her anchor. Then the sails went over, and filled on the other tack; and the racket was repeated. As the wind increased in force, the noise and shaking increased, until even the heavy sleepers in the cabin were disturbed. Bent Fillwing was the first to wake. He rushed to the companion-way, and took a look at things on deck.

The schooner was at anchor, and the jib was hauled down. He returned to the cabin, and saw

Tom fast asleep in his berth. The rest of the starboard-watch were snoring on the divan. At this moment the wind filled the fore and main sails, and the yacht heeled over till Bent could hardly stand up.

"Tom Topover!" he shouted at the top of his lungs. "You are a pretty captain!"

"What's the matter, Bent?" asked Tom, straightening himself up in his berth.

"Nothing yet, but something will soon be the matter. Is this the way you sail the schooner? You are a pretty captain, to turn in and leave the Lily to take care of herself!" raved Bent, indignant at the conduct of the captain.

"Hold your jaw, Bent Fillwing, or I will bat you over the head!" returned Tom, as soon as he came to the consciousness that he was the captain of the schooner, and that one of the crew was scolding at him. "Go on deck, and lower the sails!"

"Lower the sails! Are you going to stay here all day? It is sunrise now, and we ought to be down to Plattsburgh by this time," replied Bent.

"I am captain of this craft, and you will obey

orders," added Tom, as he turned over in his berth, as if he intended to go to sleep again.

The racket on board had aroused Pell Sankland and Kidd Digfield. Bent told them to follow him, and he went on deck. They were surprised, as Bent had been, to find the schooner at anchor under the lee of Cannon's Point. Without losing any time, and without regard to the orders of the sleepy captain, they got up the anchor, hoisted the jib, and the Lily stood away from her anchorage.

Bent put Kidd Digfield at the wheel, and then went into the cabin to "have it out" with the captain. Though he had learned all about nautical obedience on board of the Sylph, he was not inclined to practise it on the present occasion. In fact, he was disposed to be a rebel, and to bring the captain to a sense of duty. He went to Tom's berth. The chief Topover was fast asleep.

The skipper had settled on his back, with his arms spread out. Bent was on the point of taking him by the collar, to bring him to a sense of duty, — for he had lost all his respect for the dignity of the office, since the incumbent had abandoned his post, — when he saw something protruding from the vest-pocket of the sleeper.

It looked like a roll of bank-bills. Without disturbing the unconscious skipper, he laid hands upon it, and adroitly secured possession of it. He did not wait to have it out with Tom. As he had supposed when he first saw it, the object was a roll of bills. With his prize, Bent went on deck again.

CHAPTER XXVIII.

STEALING A MARCH UPON THE LEADER.

BENT FILLWING took the roll of bills from his pocket as he halted on the forecastle. He had possessed himself of the principal secret of Tom Topover, and he felt that he was in condition to dictate to his superior if he was disposed to do so. He realized that Tom was not competent to manage the schooner, and he had his doubts about his own ability.

He opened the roll of bills. The first one he saw was a ten. So was the next one, and it soon appeared that the roll of bills were all of this denomination. There were six of them, and the amount was sixty dollars. It was a large sum of money for a boy to have, and he wondered where Tom had obtained it. But it did not much matter to him, so far as the moral question was concerned. The Topover must have stolen the money, for he had no way to obtain it honestly.

But Tom had not been off the estate except in the boats; and, so far as Bent had seen, there was no money left there so that it could be stolen.

It was possible that he had robbed the room of some teacher or other person. When the loss was discovered, there would be a tremendous tempest at Beech Hill. The absence of the Lily would be discovered about the same time, and the roll would be called. They were sure to be caught. There was no end of circus and theatre in the sum of sixty dollars, to say nothing of what might be bought at the stores, or obtained at the hotels.

But the risk was tremendous. Captain Gildrock would be up by this time. It would be natural enough for him to discover the loss of the Lily, when he took his first look at Beechwater. Taking the boat was one thing, but stealing the sixty dollars was another thing, and the principal might resort to a court to settle the matter. The schooner was within four miles of Beech Hill, and many hours of the night had been wasted.

Bent was full of doubts, and he cast anxious glances up and down the lake to see if the Sylph or the Goldwing was not in pursuit of them. The wind was fresh, but not as strong as it had been on Saturday. He could not expect to escape the steamer, and hardly the Gull-wing, with her skil-ful skipper at the helm. He wished he was out of the scrape, not on moral considerations but because the risk was so great. Putting the money in his pocket he went aft and seated himself in the standing-room.

He looked at Dick and Phil. They did not appear at all as though they were having a good time. When he thought of the promised fun ahead, the theatre and the shows, he could not help seeing that any enjoyment, if there was any ahead, was to be purchased at the price of sub-mission to Tom Topover. He was carrying it with a high hand, and sailed under "sealed orders."

"Do you think there is any fun ahead for us, Bill?" he asked, after he had thought of the sit-uation for a while.

"I don't see any. I supposed we should be off Plattsburgh or a good way farther north than we are; and it looks more as though we should be caught than that we should have a time," replied Bill.

"We have nothing to eat on board," added Phil. "There may be some crackers, or some-

[illegible] of that sort; but we shall get no breakfast unless we land at Burlington."

"[illegible] do you know that we will be able to land at Burlington?" asked [illegible]. "[illegible] the tide [illegible] in the bay."

"If we want to land there we can do it; for we [illegible] half of the party, and we are as good as the other half," replied Ben.

"We haven't any money to pay a breakfast, if we should land while Tom is asleep," added Paul. "It will be a starving time, and I am sick of it. I didn't wish to come, and I am sorry now that Tom beat me into it."

"I have been sorry I came, ever since I got into the [illegible]. Tom never used to be so ugly, and now he treats us as though we were his [illegible]."

"Precisely so; and as you say, I have had [illegible] enough of it," said Ben. "I expect to see the Sylph at the Goldwing pier [illegible] before we can get to Burlington, if we are going there," and Ben looked up the lake again.

"We can't [illegible] any thing [illegible] short of [illegible], and then than waiting till we can get to Plattsburgh," remarked Paul. "I know Tom won't let us go ashore at Burlington; so that we are not likely to get any thing to eat till noon, if we are not caught before that time. Tom has the money, and he can starve us if we don't mind him."

Bent Fillwing pulled the roll of bills from his pocket, and held it up before his companions. He explained how he had obtained it; and, for some little time, they wondered where Tom got the money.

"Now, fellows, there are only two things that we can do," said Bent, who had evidently come to a conclusion. "We have money enough to buy a breakfast in Burlington; but we wear a uniform, and everybody will know us as soon as we show our coats and caps. Captain Gildrock has found out before this time that the Lily is gone. It is about six o'clock now, and he can ascertain who have taken her by looking out for the absent students. It would be like him to telegraph to Burlington to have us arrested, or to have the boat captured if we don't go on shore. It will be hot water ahead, whatever we do."

"I am in favor of going back to Beech Hill," said Kidd Digfield. "If I had known the Lily was at anchor, I should have taken one of the boats and gone ashore, or pulled back to the school."

"I was ready to go with him," added Pell Sank·land. "We have been well used at the school; and there is ten times as much fun there as there is going off on a time as the slaves of Tom Topover."

"Shall we put about, and go to Beech Hill?" asked Bent.

"I am in favor of it," replied Kidd, and Pell agreed with him.

Kidd was the best sailor of the three; and he was allowed to retain the wheel, and direct the movements of the others. Without any difficulty, he brought the Lily on her course to the southward. The wind was freshening all the time, and the sea was beginning to look very rough in the broad lake ahead of them.

"We shall have a sweet row as soon as Tom Topover wakes up," said Bent, when they had all resumed their places in the standing-room. "But I don't care for that. Don't say a word about the money; and, as soon as we get to Beech Hill, I will hand it over to Captain Gildrock."

"Not a word," replied Kidd. "Tom is sure to pitch into us as soon as he finds that we are headed for Beech Hill."

"He will take the schooner away from us, and head her the other way," added Pell.

"I don't believe he will," replied Bent, shaking his head as though he meant business. "There are three of us; and I will agree to take care of Tom, if you will take care of the others. One of us ought to take the lead; and you may as well do so, Kidd."

"I would rather have you do that; though I will handle the schooner as well as I can, if you will prevent Tom from interfering with me," answered Kidd.

"I will do that," Bent assented; and he did not seem to think he had taken a large contract.

"Tom Topover could lick any fellow in Genverres, and all of us used to be afraid of him," said Pell.

"Since Dory Dornwood knocked him out, and Paul Bristol gave him more than he could stomach, the fellows have not been afraid of him. Ash Burton and Sam Spottwood were ready to stand up before him."

"I am not afraid of him," added Bent, who had been another such fellow as Tom, in the town where he lived.

All these boys had been greatly influenced, and their characters modified, by their residence at Beech Hill. Now that the three on deck had taken the first step towards putting themselves right, they found a certain strength which had not belonged to them before. They had taken their position, and they were ready to carry it out in spite of the blows and the ridicule of Tom. The two original Topovers were beginning to understand why they had yielded to their old leader, but the fear of his sharp sarcasm had been over-come.

The Lily sailed like a bird, having the wind nearly on the beam. It was only four miles to the mouth of the river, with a leading wind all the way up to the moorings. While they were talking, they heard a distant church-clock strike six. They had got under way before five, and now they were close to the mouth of the river.

Tom still slept; for he had been very tired, and he had been up till a very late hour for him. The motion of the schooner was very easy, and Bent had closed the doors of the cabin so that the conversation could not be heard if any one waked below. After the Lily had come about, she had held a straight course to the river. Not a sheet had been disturbed, and not much change would be required until she reached the bend in the outlet of Beechwater. Kidd had advised that no noise should be made, for he wished to postpone as long as possible the row with Tom Topover.

The result of his cautionary measures resulted much better than he could have anticipated. The Lily went into the river, and the increasing breeze went with her. With a south-west wind, there was no difficulty at the bend; though it was necessary to gybe her there. The wind was not strong enough yet to make this a very dangerous manœuvre; and she came about handsomely, and the mainsail was eased off so that it made but little noise.

"Here we are!" exclaimed Bent in a low tone, when the schooner shot into Beechwater. "There will be no row after all; or, if there is, the principal can settle it. I hope we shall be able to get ashore before Tom wakes."

"Then, if you will get the anchor ready, we

will ease it into the water, and haul the jib down without noise," added Kidd.

"We have stolen a march upon Tom, and I hope we shall get ashore without waking him," said Pell, as he went forward with Bent.

At the right time Kidd luffed her up, and went forward to assist in the work there. He hauled down the jib while his companions were easing the anchor into the water. In a moment she was fast to the bottom. Tom had not yet put in an appearance, and the rebels had succeeded beyond their expectations.

"Don't go aft again," said Kidd, as he hauled the skiff up to the bow of the schooner. He had preferred to anchor, lest the noise of mooring should disturb the sleepers.

Bent got into the skiff, and was followed by the others. They paddled to the shore, and left the Lily with her fore and main sail set. They landed at the old wharf. As they had supposed, the principal was wide awake, and had discovered the loss of the Lily. He had called the students together, and had only just taken the names of the absent ones. When he saw the Lily come into Beechwater, he walked at once to the old wharf.

"Good-morning, Digfield! Good-morning, Fill-wing! You have been taking an early sail," said the principal in his usual tones.

Bent replied to the salutation, and then handed the roll of bills to Captain Gildrock, who received them with astonishment, not to say wonder.

CHAPTER XXIX.

TOM TOPOVER'S RECEPTION.

"SIXTY dollars! " exclaimed Captain Gildrock, when he had looked over the roll of bills handed him by Bent Fillwing. "Why do you give this money to me?"

"Doesn't it belong to you, sir?" asked Bent, who had put on the meekest expression he could find among his resources.

"I am not aware that it does. I have not lost any money," added the principal.

"Has any one about the school lost any, sir?" inquired Bent, who began to think he had proceeded too rapidly.

"I have not heard of any one who has lost any money. Perhaps you had better explain where you got it, as you seem to be anxious to get rid of it," suggested the captain.

"We went on a little lark in the Lily, but some

of us concluded to bring her back," replied Bent, fixing his gaze upon the ground, which is the proper thing for a penitent to do.

"Where is Tom Topover, who went with you?" asked the principal, as he looked at the three excursionists who had presented themselves before him. "Where are Splugger and Dumper?"

"We left them asleep on board of the Lily," replied Bent, with a smile, as he watched the expression of the principal. "As they don't show themselves, I suppose they are still asleep."

Bent Fillwing chuckled when he thought of the trick he had played on Tom Topover. He had expected a fight with him, and he had even been ready for that; for he did not believe so much in the pugilistic prowess of the bully as most of the students, and he was at home in that sort of business. He thought he knew how to manage the principal; and he was acting all the time, as much as though he had been the leading card in a show.

The story of Ash Burton and Sam Spottwood, who had escaped the consequences of the stealing of the Goldwing, was well known; and the principal seemed to have a weakness in the direction of penitents, if he had one in any direction. It was evident that he knew all about the scrape as far as it could be ascertained at Beech Hill, for he had mentioned all the names of the party not before him.

"You seem to be amused at something, Fillwing," continued Captain Gildrock, smiling himself.

"We have concluded to tell the whole truth, and keep nothing back, not even the money," said Bent; though he had a sort of suspicion that he had been a little premature in disposing so suddenly of the sixty dollars.

"That is a wise plan. It seems that you have voluntarily returned, in spite of Tom Topover, Splugger, and Dumper," replied the principal encouragingly.

"Yes, sir, we were sure we should be captured; and, while Tom was asleep, we brought him back to Beech Hill, and we are very sorry we took any part in the enterprise," added Bent, acting his part very well; though the principal understood him as well as though he had said he was playing the penitent.

"Perhaps it is fortunate for you that he was asleep, if you decided to retrace your steps."

"I think we should have come back all the same if he had been awake, though it might have cost us a fight in that case; and we had agreed to take things as they came," replied Bent, with a modest display of virtue.

"That is, you had resolved to fight for the privilege of doing your duty," added Captain Gildrock. "Don't be over modest about it. Duty presented herself before you; and, though peril and suffering lay between you and her, you were determined to follow her at all hazards."

This raillery took all the starch out of Bent Fillwing. The principal saw through his parade of confession, and took no stock in his penitence.

"I said we came back because we were sure we should be caught, though we all agreed that the scrape was a bad egg," replied Bent, switching off to a new track.

"What was the scrape?" asked the captain, looking from one to another of the delinquents.

"That is more than we know. Tom Topover sailed under sealed orders; and he would not tell us what we were going to do, or where we were going. He promised us that we should go to the theatre, and live at the hotels; and he did not mean to come back to Beech Hill. We couldn't get any thing out of him in regard to his plan. He said he would pay the bills, but he would not tell us any thing," Bent explained.

"And you went with him on these terms?"

"I was willing enough to go, until he put on as many airs as though he had been the principal of the Beech-Hill Industrial School. He was always under sealed orders, and gave off his commands as though he expected them to be obeyed, and no questions asked."

"That is the proper way to obey orders," added the principal, with a smile.

"Kidd and Pell did not want to go, but Tom blackguarded them into joining; and they were ready enough to come back as soon as the way was open. I don't know but they would have had a fight in order to follow that lady you spoke of," continued Bent, who was himself now.

"What lady? I have spoken of no lady."

"Duty — Miss Duty; but she was not as good-looking as Miss Lily Bristol. In our case she seemed to be pointing to the door of the brig."

The principal thought he might get the truth out of Kidd Digfield and Pell Sankland, who had not yet spoken a word. He questioned them; and they told him without any attempt at concealment or palliation, and with no mock humility, all that had occurred since they went to their rooms the night before. They were genuine penitents, and there was no fraud about them.

"You were weak to allow the blackguard talk of a fellow like Tom Topover to turn you aside, but you will know better next time," added Captain Gildrock very mildly. "Do you know any thing about this money?"

"Nothing at all, sir: I did not know Tom had it, except from what he said," replied Kidd.

"You don't know where he got it?"

Not one of them had the remotest idea.

"I came to the conclusion that he had robbed some teacher's room, or had been exploring your strong-box, sir," interposed Bent. "At any rate, I was sure that he had not come honestly by it; and, when I saw it sticking out of his pocket, I took possession of it, for it was the sinews of war."

"And, when you got it, you decided to return?" asked the principal, with a smile.

Bent winced under the glance bestowed upon

him; for he realized that the principal understood him, and that any more humility or pretence of duty would do him no good.

"I did not decide to return because I had got .the money, but because Tom had deserted his post, and instead of being up at Plattsburgh, or some point miles nearer the foot of the lake, we were not four miles from the mouth of Beaver River."

"That sounds quite reasonable. Tom had spoiled the enterprise he had undertaken to manage," added the captain.

"That was exactly it. He was sleepy, and then he anchored the schooner and turned in. I knew we couldn't get away after he had lost three or four hours. There was no chance for us, and I gave it up as soon as I had looked over the ground. The moment I said a word, Kidd and Pell were eager to come back."

"You may come over to the boat-house with me," continued the principal, leading the way.

The boat-house was open, and they found all the students assembled there. The smoke was pouring out of the smoke-stack of the Sylph, and the runaways concluded that they were getting her ready to go in search of the Lily. No one seemed to be stirring yet on board of the schooner; and it was evident that Tom Topover and his two companions had not yet finished their nap. It was only seven o'clock, and they had not turned in till one; so that they had not yet made up the eight hours of sleep to which they were accustomed.

Dory Dornwood and Paul Bristol were called by Captain Gildrock, and directed to go out to the Lily, buoy the cable without waiting to get up the anchor, and to bring her to the wharf without waking those in the cabin.

Dory laughed heartily when he had learned enough of the absence of the schooner to comprehend the situation; and he and Paul executed the order with which they were charged, to the letter. The Lily was brought alongside of the wharf, and made fast. The sleepers in the cabin were entering on their seventh hour of slumber, and the movements of the boat had not disturbed them.

"Now, boys, form a line," said the principal. "Keep step; and, when I give the word, I want you to put your feet down in earnest."

The students formed the line; and, when Bent and his two associates held back, they were required to take their places in the line. The boys had been trained a little in a few military movements for marching purposes, and they knew how to place themselves. Dory was directed to lead them to the deck of the Lily; and the students were required to step lightly, until the word was given for a change.

The students filed upon the deck of the schooner, in good order, and without making any noise. When the last one was on the deck, and Dory had marched the head of the column around the standing-room, Captain Gildrock gave the word, "Attention! march!" The file was closed up, so that the students stood touching each other. All as one, they began to put their feet down on the planks in a very heavy step. All hands were intensely amused, for they had been told the situation of things on board, and were laughing as though they enjoyed the affair in which they were engaged. Tom and his fellow-rebels would have no reason to suppose they were not at anchor off Cannon's Point.

The tramp of their feet could be heard half a mile from the wharf, for Mrs. Bristol and Lily soon came to the scene to ascertain what the matter was. The boys kept up the step with all the vigor of those interested in the business. The cabin-doors were closed ; but, if the runaways were still alive, they could not help waking, with such a tremendous noise over their heads.

"On deck there! what are you doing?" shouted Tom Topover, at the top of his lungs. "What's all that noise for?"

The principal, who still stood on the wharf, where he could overlook the operations, raised his hand ; and all the students became as statues at once. Silence reigned supreme. In a low tone, he told Dory to be ready to give three cheers; and the word was passed along the line.

"Why don't you answer me, Bent Fillwing?" shouted Tom again, when no attention was paid to his first call.

The silence was not broken, and Tom was evidently getting mad. A moment later he pushed open the cabin-doors, and tumbled out into the standing-room.

"Three cheers!" exclaimed Dory, prompted by his uncle.

The cheers were lustily given, and Tom opened his eyes very wide.

"THE PRINCIPAL STOOD ON THE WHARF, WHERE HE COULD OVERLOOK
THE OPERATIONS."—PAGE 326.

CHAPTER XXX.

THE REFORMED TOPOVERS AT BEECH HILL.

WHEN Tom Topover heard the cheers, he had made his way into the standing-room. He had evidently expected to find his turbulent subordinate, Bent Fillwing, there; and he had opened his mouth to give him a severe rating. But when he saw the students of the school gathered around in solid phalanx, he started back, and looked as though he had seen the world suddenly come to an end.

He had slept like a log; and he had not the remotest suspicion that the Lily was not at anchor off Cannon's Point, where he had left her the night before. A remarkable change had taken place in the situation, and he could not account for it. He saw that the Lily was at the wharf; and there was the boat-house; and on the edge of the wharf stood the principal, looking as smiling as though no case of discipline ever troubled him.

Nim Splugger and Jack Dumper had been awakened by the tramp of the boys on deck, and were at the heels of the chief when he went up the companion-way to the standing-room. They were quite as much astonished as Tom. In fact, all three of them were utterly confounded by the situation. If they had been dreaming, in their heavy slumber, of the theatre and circus, — visits to which had been confidently promised to them, — they awoke to a terrible certainty that the fun was all over.

The principal said nothing for a couple of minutes, in order to allow Tom and his companions to take it all in, and gather up their ideas. Then he stepped down from the wharf, and took a stand on the rail of the schooner.

"Good-morning, Captain Topover; for I understand that you are the commander of this schooner," the principal began, with mock solemnity. "We learned that you had arrived this morning, in your fine craft; and we have turned out to give you a fitting reception. When great men come to Beech Hill, we do our best to receive them with suitable honors.

"On your return from your cruise in the Lily,

it gives us great pleasure to welcome you. We hardly expected to see you so soon; and your arrival at this early hour deprives the students of the pleasure of meeting you on the lake in the Sylph, in which they were preparing to receive you some time in the course of the day.

"We congratulate you on the happy circumstance that you have brought the Lily back in good condition, and we have no doubt you have enjoyed your excursion very much. We understand that you have enforced discipline on board of the schooner; and, as you were sailing under sealed orders, you have kept your own counsel. For myself, I may say that I have received the sixty dollars which was the sinews of the trip."

"I didn't steal that money," blubbered Tom, as he looked at the principal, and realized that all the students, even to Bent, Kidd, and Pell, who were seen among them, were laughing at him, and enjoying the scene to their hearts' content.

"My dear Captain Topover, no one has accused you of stealing it!" exclaimed the principal. "You sailed under sealed orders, and you did not even tell your companions in the enterprise where you got that money. This was all very proper, for it takes away from the dignity of a commander to be too familiar with his subordinates. We look upon you as a mighty man, and we hardly expect you to be more communicative to us."

Tom seemed to be a little bothered at the allusion to the money, and he began to feel in his vest-pocket for the bills. He had not shown them to his companions; and they could not have known any thing about the money, except the hint he had given them that he was provided with funds. The roll of bills had been in his pocket when he went to sleep: it was not there now. And the principal was talking about the amount, which he had not mentioned, to the whole school. It looked very strange to him now that he had time to collect his thoughts. He could not explain it. „

At this point of the interview, the breakfast-bell rang at the door of the mansion.

"It is a happy circumstance that you arrived just in time for our morning meal, and we shall take great pleasure in escorting you to the banquet hall. You must have an appetite after the labors of the night, most of which you have spent in your berth," continued Captain Gildrock.

"March to the house by twos, and open ranks in the middle to receive our distinguished guests on this occasion."

The students doubled up, and marched ashore. In the middle of the column, in single file, the three rebels were placed. Tom did not know what to make of it. If the principal or Bates had taken him by the collar, and pitched him on the deck, he could have comprehended it. If he was disposed to rebel, he could not do so in the face of the ridicule that was in process of being heaped upon him. He took his place in the line, and the column marched to the house.

The teachers and others had collected on the lawn, aware that something unusual had transpired; and they could not help joining in the general laugh, when they saw in the procession the three runaways marching to the mansion. At the table all took their usual places, and the lake voyagers were hungry enough to do excellent justice to the meal set before them.

While they were at breakfast, Bates moved the Lily back to her moorings, fished up the anchor, and put the craft in her usual neat trim. Nothing was said at the table about the escapade of the

Topover party; and, though the students kept an eye on the chief, the principal hardly glanced at him. While he was still at the head of the table, a servant brought in the morning mail. As the party rose from their seats, the captain handed the letters to those to whom they were directed. Among several belonging to himself, he opened one. He read for a moment, and then rapped on the table.

"Here is a letter from a gentleman who was here to see me yesterday; and, as it explains a great mystery, I will read a portion of it to you, as it relates to the sinews of the late cruise of the Lily. 'On my return from Beech Hill last evening, I went to the office of the Van Ness House to pay my bill, for I intended to go home by the evening train; but I found I had not a dollar in my pocket. I had a roll of bills in my vest-pocket, which, to the best of my remembrance, contained sixty dollars. I have not the least idea where I lost it. Possibly, I dropped it in your grounds. If so, and you happen to find it, please give me credit for the amount, or send a check to me at my residence; for I borrowed enough to get home with.'

"Now, thanks to the honesty of Captain Topover, late commander of the Lily in her cruise to,
but not from, Cannon's Point, I am enabled to return this money to its rightful owner," continued
the principal. "It has been placed in my hands
for safe keeping, and I did not expect to find
the owner of it so soon."

"Who placed it in your hands for safe keeping?" asked Tom, rather impudently.

"I think we will follow your example, — sail
under sealed orders, and keep our own counsel,"
replied Captain Gildrock. "At any rate, none of
the money will be spent for theatre and circus,
and none for hotel-bills on our account."

The students laughed heartily at the discomfit-
ure of Tom Topover. Captain Gildrock had told
the three penitents not to mention the manner in
which the money had been obtained, or that they
had handed it to him. He did not care to have
Tom pick a quarrel with Bent on account of it.
This part of the adventure remained concealed
from all, and Tom could not explain it; though he
suspected that his three renegade companions had
done some things which they did not explain.

The students went to their studies, and the

rebels were surprised that nothing more was said to them. The only penalty to which they were subjected was that the windows were covered with bars again, in the rooms of Tom, Nim, and Jack Dumper. The others were truly sorry for the part they had played in the scrape, and no punishment awaited them. But the ridicule to which the three guilty ones were subjected, proved to be a very salutary medicine for their complaint.

"You went back on me, Bent Fillwing," said Tom Topover, in the evening, when they were alone on the lawn.

"And you went back on the whole of us," retorted Bent.

"I did? Not a bit of it! If you hadn't deserted me, I would have done all I promised. What do you mean by saying that I went back on you? Tom Topover never went back on any fellow in his life."

"Bosh!" sneered Bent. "When you got sleepy, you anchored the schooner and went to sleep. I call that going back on us in the worst possible manner. You haven't brains enough to manage any affair, Tom Topover. You are as vain as a bantam rooster, and you put on airs enough to fit out a sergeant at a country muster."

"None of your lip, Bent Fillwing. If you talk like that, I'll bat you over the head. I don't let any fellow talk to me like that," said Tom, doubling up his fists.

"You will let me tell you the truth; or I will tell you, whether you let me or not. If you want to bat me over the head, I will show you, in one second after you have done it, how long you are when you are spread out on the ground. I repeat, that you are a vain pup, and no fellow can trust you. When Kidd and Pell and I had the watch below, what did you do on deck? You gave up the battle, and went to sleep. In the morning, when we ought to have been below Burlington, and out of sight of people who know us, we were fast to the anchor, only four miles from the mouth of the river. I had no confidence in you, and I gave it up. I wouldn't trust you to lead a farrow hen to water."

"You and I will have to settle this business, Bent Fillwing," muttered Tom.

"Why don't you settle it now, if you want to. If you wish to know how long you are, I can

make a plan of you on the ground in the twin·
kling of an eye. Then you acted as though you
were the commander of a big man-of-war, when
you were nothing but a sick puppy. No fellow
could stand it when you began to lord it over
him. If we had not brought the schooner back,
the Sylph would have captured us; and then the
fun would have been all over. It was no use to
think of doing any thing, after you had lost four
hours of the time we ought to have used in getting
to a safe part of the lake."

"How did old Gildrock get that sixty dollars?"
asked Tom, finding it was useless to bully Bent.
He was too ready to be hit, and to return the
compliment.

"Don't you suppose he went down to your
berth after you came into Beechwater, and took
it from your pocket?" asked Bent, laughing.

Tom did not believe he had done so. But he
could get nothing out of him or the other penitents, and he had to give it up. Perhaps he will
know some day, but it is still a great mystery to
him.

Captain Gildrock said it was a great misfortune
to Tom, that he had found that roll of bills. The

money had, no doubt, tempted him to plan the excursion in the Lily, on the spur of the moment. He would not have thought of such a thing, if the " sinews " had not been obtained by accident.

Up to this time, Tom had been doing very well. He observed all the rules, and learned his lessons. In the shop he was particularly attentive to his work. For some time before the long vacation the students had been engaged in building the engine for the proposed steamer, which was to be about half the size of the Sylph. Tom was employed on this work, and his lessons related to the natural forces employed to obtain steam-power. He was interested in this subject, and he read with attention all his text-book contained in relation to it.

In a few weeks, when it was seen that Tom and his associates in the cruise of the Lily were doing as well as they knew how, the bars were removed from their windows, and the doors were not locked at night. All of them were allowed to visit their parents, and to spend Sunday with them; but they did not value the privilege very highly, and preferred to spend most of the time at Beech Hill.

Tom became a skilful machinist in time, though he never entirely recovered from the faults of his disposition. He was kept busy at the school during his three years; and he gave but little trouble, on the whole, though he sometimes had an outbreak which worked off the bad blood for the time. The people of Genverres were astonished at the fact, when they realized it, that the Topovers had been reformed, and were doing their duty in the institution. It was a merciful thing to them as well as to the boys, for they had suffered a great deal from their pranks and depredations.

Mrs. Sankland had occasion to look back to the fire in her house as a godsend; for it had called the attention of the people to her wants, and she was supplied with all the work she could do.

About the time Tom Topover graduated, and took a place to run a stationary engine, his father died; and he did his full share in supporting the family. The school had made a new man of him, as a school of no other kind could have done.

A little later in the season, the keel of the steam-yacht was laid down in the sheds built for the accommodation of the Lily. The wood-workers among the students labored on her all winter, and had enough to do; while those in the metal-shops finished the engine.

In the following spring, as soon as the weather was suitable for going out on the lake, classes in boat-sailing were organized, under the instruction of Matt Randolph and Dory Dornwood, who continued in service as captains of the Lily and the Goldwing; and all hands made a practical use of the phrase they had so often heard, "Ready, about!" as they learned the art of "sailing the boat."

OLIVER OPTIC'S BOOKS

All-Over-the-World Library. By OLIVER OPTIC. First Series. Illustrated. Price per volume, $1.25.

1. **A Missing Million;** OR, THE ADVENTURES OF LOUIS BELGRADE.
2. **A Millionaire at Sixteen;** OR, THE CRUISE OF THE " GUARDIAN MOTHER."
3. **A Young Knight Errant;** OR, CRUISING IN THE WEST INDIES.
4. **Strange Sights Abroad;** OR, ADVENTURES IN EUROPEAN WATERS.

No author has come before the public during the present generation who has achieved a larger and more deserving popularity among young people than " Oliver Optic." His stories have been very numerous, but they have been uniformly excellent in moral tone and literary quality. As indicated in the general title, it is the author's intention to conduct the readers of this entertaining series " around the world." As a means to this end, the hero of the story purchases a steamer which he names the " Guardian Mother," and with a number of guests she proceeds on her voyage. — *Christian Work, N. Y.*

All-Over-the-World Library. By OLIVER OPTIC. Second Series. Illustrated. Price per volume, $1.25.

1. **American Boys Afloat;** OR, CRUISING IN THE ORIENT.
2. **The Young Navigators;** OR, THE FOREIGN CRUISE OF THE " MAUD."
3. **Up and Down the Nile;** OR, YOUNG ADVENTURERS IN AFRICA.
4. **Asiatic Breezes;** OR, STUDENTS ON THE WING.

The interest in these stories is continuous, and there is a great variety of exciting incident woven into the solid information which the book imparts so generously and without the slightest suspicion of dryness. Manly boys will welcome this volume as cordially as they did its predecessors. — *Boston Gazette.*

All-Over-the-World Library. By OLIVER OPTIC. Third Series. Illustrated. Price per volume, $1.25.

1. **Across India;** OR, LIVE BOYS IN THE FAR EAST.
2. **Half Round the World;** OR, AMONG THE UNCIVILIZED.
3. **Four Young Explorers;** OR, SIGHT-SEEING IN THE TROPICS.
4. **Pacific Shores;** OR, ADVENTURES IN EASTERN SEAS.

Amid such new and varied surroundings it would be surprising indeed if the author, with his faculty of making even the commonplace attractive, did not tell an intensely interesting story of adventure, as well as give much information in regard to the distant countries through which our friends pass, and the strange peoples with whom they are brought in contact. This book, and indeed the whole series, is admirably adapted to reading aloud in the family circle, each volume containing matter which will interest all the members of the family. — *Boston Budget.*

OLIVER OPTIC'S BOOKS

The Famous Boat Club Series. By OLIVER OPTIC. Six volumes. Illustrated. Any volume sold separately. Price per volume $1.25.

1. **The Boat Club**; OR, THE BUNKERS OF RIPPLETON.
2. **All Aboard**; OR, LIFE ON THE LAKE.
3. **Now or Never**; OR, THE ADVENTURES OF BOBBY BRIGHT.
4. **Try Again**; OR, THE TRIALS AND TRIUMPHS OF HARRY WEST.
5. **Poor and Proud**; OR, THE FORTUNES OF KATY REDBURN.
6. **Little by Little**; OR, THE CRUISE OF THE FLYAWAY.

"This is the first series of books written for the young by OLIVER OPTIC. It laid the foundation for his fame as the first of authors in which the young delight, and gained for him the title of the Prince of Story Tellers. The six books are varied in incident and plot, but all are entertaining and original."

(Other volumes in preparation.)

Young America Abroad: A LIBRARY OF TRAVEL AND ADVENTURE IN FOREIGN LANDS. By OLIVER OPTIC. Illustrated by NAST and others. First Series. Six volumes. Any volume sold separately. Price per volume, $1.25.

1. **Outward Bound**; OR, YOUNG AMERICA AFLOAT.
2. **Shamrock and Thistle**; OR, YOUNG AMERICA IN IRELAND AND SCOTLAND.
3. **Red Cross**; OR, YOUNG AMERICA IN ENGLAND AND WALES.
4. **Dikes and Ditches**; OR, YOUNG AMERICA IN HOLLAND AND BELGIUM.
5. **Palace and Cottage**; OR, YOUNG AMERICA IN FRANCE AND SWITZERLAND.
6. **Down the Rhine**; OR, YOUNG AMERICA IN GERMANY.

"The story from its inception, and through the twelve volumes (see Second Series), is a bewitching one, while the information imparted concerning the countries of Europe and the isles of the sea is not only correct in every particular, but is told in a captivating style. OLIVER OPTIC will continue to be the boys' friend, and his pleasant books will continue to be read by thousands of American boys. What a fine holiday present either or both series of ' Young America Abroad' would be for a young friend! It would make a little library highly prized by the recipient, and would not be an expensive one."—*Providence Press.*

Young America Abroad. By OLIVER OPTIC. Second Series. Six volumes. Illustrated. Any volume sold separately. Price per volume, $1.25.

1. **Up the Baltic**; OR, YOUNG AMERICA IN NORWAY, SWEDEN, AND DENMARK.
2. **Northern Lands**; OR, YOUNG AMERICA IN RUSSIA AND PRUSSIA.
3. **Cross and Crescent**; OR, YOUNG AMERICA IN TURKEY AND GREECE.
4. **Sunny Shores**; OR, YOUNG AMERICA IN ITALY AND AUSTRIA.
5. **Vine and Olive**; OR, YOUNG AMERICA IN SPAIN AND PORTUGAL.
6. **Isles of the Sea**; OR, YOUNG AMERICA HOMEWARD BOUND.

"OLIVER OPTIC is a *nom de plume* that is known and loved by almost every boy of intelligence in the land. We have seen a highly intellectual and world-weary man, a cynic whose heart was somewhat embittered by its large experience of human nature, take up one of OLIVER OPTIC's books, and read it at a sitting, neglecting his work in yielding to the fascination of the pages. When a mature and exceedingly well-informed mind, long despoiled of all its freshness, can thus find pleasure in a book for boys, no additional words of recommendation are needed."—*Sunday Times.*

OLIVER OPTIC'S BOOKS

The Blue and the Gray—Afloat. By OLIVER OPTIC. Six volumes. Illustrated. Beautiful binding in blue and gray, with emblematic dies. Cloth. Any volume sold separately. Price per volume, $1.50.

1. Taken by the Enemy.
2. Within the Enemy's Lines.
3. On the Blockade.
4. Stand by the Union.
5. Fighting for the Right.
6. A Victorious Union.

The Blue and the Gray—on Land.

1. Brother against Brother.
2. In the Saddle.
3. A Lieutenant at Eighteen.
4. On the Staff.
5. At the Front.

(Volume Six in preparation.)

"There never has been a more interesting writer in the field of juvenile literature than Mr. W. T. ADAMS, who, under his well-known pseudonym, is known and admired by every boy and girl in the country, and by thousands who have long since passed the boundaries of youth, yet who remember with pleasure the genial, interesting pen that did so much to interest, instruct, and entertain their younger years. 'The Blue and the Gray' is a title that is sufficiently indicative of the nature and spirit of the latest series, while the name of OLIVER OPTIC is sufficient warrant of the absorbing style of narrative. This series is as bright and entertaining as any work that Mr. ADAMS has yet put forth, and will be as eagerly perused as any that has borne his name. It would not be fair to the prospective reader to deprive him of the zest which comes from the unexpected by entering into a synopsis of the story. A word, however, should be said in regard to the beauty and appropriateness of the binding, which makes it a most attractive volume."—*Boston Budget.*

Woodville Stories. By OLIVER OPTIC. Six volumes. Illustrated. Any volume sold separately. Price per volume, $1.25.

1. Rich and Humble; OR, THE MISSION OF BERTHA GRANT.
2. In School and Out; OR, THE CONQUEST OF RICHARD GRANT.
3. Watch and Wait; OR, THE YOUNG FUGITIVES.
4. Work and Win; OR, NODDY NEWMAN ON A CRUISE.
5. Hope and Have; OR, FANNY GRANT AMONG THE INDIANS
6. Haste and Waste; OR, THE YOUNG PILOT OF LAKE CHAMPLAIN

"Though we are not so young as we once were, we relished these stories almost as much as the boys and girls for whom they were written. They were really refreshing, even to us. There is much in them which is calculated to inspire a generous, healthy ambition, and to make distasteful all reading tending to stimulate base desires."—*Fitchburg Reveille.*

The Starry Flag Series. By OLIVER OPTIC. In six volumes. Illustrated. Any volume sold separately. Price per volume, $1.25.

1. The Starry Flag; OR, THE YOUNG FISHERMAN OF CAPE ANN.
2. Breaking Away; OR, THE FORTUNES OF A STUDENT.
3. Seek and Find; OR, THE ADVENTURES OF A SMART BOY.
4. Freaks of Fortune; OR, HALF ROUND THE WORLD.
5. Make or Break; OR, THE RICH MAN'S DAUGHTER.
6. Down the River; OR, BUCK BRADFORD AND THE TYRANTS.

"Mr. ADAMS, the celebrated and popular writer, familiarly known as OLIVER OPTIC, seems to have inexhaustible funds for weaving together the virtues of life; and, notwithstanding he has written scores of books, the same freshness and novelty run through them all. Some people think the sensational element predominates. Perhaps it does. But a book for young people needs this, and so long as good sentiments are inculcated such books ought to be read."

LEE AND SHEPARD, BOSTON, SEND THEIR COMPLETE CATALOGUE FREE.

OLIVER OPTIC'S BOOKS

The Great Western Series. By OLIVER OPTIC. In six volumes. Illustrated. Any volume sold separately. Price per volume, $1.25.

1. **Going West;** OR, THE PERILS OF A POOR BOY.
2. **Out West;** OR, ROUGHING IT ON THE GREAT LAKES.
3. **Lake Breezes;** OR, THE CRUISE OF THE SYLVANIA.
4. **Going South;** OR, YACHTING ON THE ATLANTIC COAST.
5. **Down South;** OR, YACHT ADVENTURES IN FLORIDA.
6. **Up the River;** OR, YACHTING ON THE MISSISSIPPI.

"This is the latest series of books issued by this popular writer, and deals with life on the Great Lakes, for which a careful study was made by the author in a summer tour of the immense water sources of America. The story, which carries the same hero through the six books of the series, is always entertaining, novel scenes and varied incidents giving a constantly changing yet always attractive aspect to the narrative. OLIVER OPTIC has written nothing better."

The Yacht Club Series. By OLIVER OPTIC. In six volumes. Illustrated. Any volume sold separately. Price per volume, $1.25.

1. **Little Bobtail;** OR, THE WRECK OF THE PENOBSCOT.
2. **The Yacht Club;** OR, THE YOUNG BOAT BUILDERS.
3. **Money-Maker;** OR, THE VICTORY OF THE BASILISK.
4. **The Coming Wave;** OR, THE TREASURE OF HIGH ROCK.
5. **The Dorcas Club;** OR, OUR GIRLS AFLOAT.
6. **Ocean Born;** OR, THE CRUISE OF THE CLUBS.

"The series has this peculiarity, that all of its constituent volumes are independent of one another, and therefore each story is complete in itself. OLIVER OPTIC is, perhaps, the favorite author of the boys and girls of this country, and he seems destined to enjoy an endless popularity. He deserves his success, for he makes very interesting stories, and inculcates none but the best sentiments, and the 'Yacht Club' is no exception to this rule."—*New Haven Journal and Courier.*

Onward and Upward Series. By OLIVER OPTIC. In six volumes. Illustrated. Any volume sold separately. Price per volume, $1.25.

1. **Field and Forest;** OR, THE FORTUNES OF A FARMER.
2. **Plane and Plank;** OR, THE MISHAPS OF A MECHANIC.
3. **Desk and Debit;** OR, THE CATASTROPHES OF A CLERK.
4. **Cringle and Crosstree;** OR, THE SEA SWASHES OF A SAILOR.
5. **Bivouac and Battle;** OR, THE STRUGGLES OF A SOLDIER.
6. **Sea and Shore;** OR, THE TRAMPS OF A TRAVELLER.

"Paul Farringford, the hero of these tales, is, like most of this author's heroes, a young man of high spirit, and of high aims and correct principles, appearing in the different volumes as a farmer, a captain, a bookkeeper, a soldier, a sailor, and a traveller. In all of them the hero meets with very exciting adventures, told in the graphic style for which the author is famous."

The Lake Shore Series. By OLIVER OPTIC. In six volumes. Illustrated. Any volume sold separately. Price per volume, $1.25.

1. **Through by Daylight;** OR, THE YOUNG ENGINEER OF THE LAKE SHORE RAILROAD.
2. **Lightning Express;** OR, THE RIVAL ACADEMIES.
3. **On Time;** OR, THE YOUNG CAPTAIN OF THE UCAYGA STEAMER.
4. **Switch Off;** OR, THE WAR OF THE STUDENTS.
5. **Brake Up;** OR, THE YOUNG PEACEMAKERS.
6. **Bear and Forbear;** OR, THE YOUNG SKIPPER OF LAKE UCAYGA.

"OLIVER OPTIC is one of the most fascinating writers for youth, and withal one of the best to be found in this or any past age. Troops of young people hang over his vivid pages; and not one of them ever learned to be mean, ignoble, cowardly, selfish, or to yield to any vice from anything they ever read from his pen."—*Providence Press.*

OLIVER OPTIC'S BOOKS

Army and Navy Stories. By OLIVER OPTIC. Six volumes. Illustrated. Any volume sold separately. Price per volume, $1.25.

1. The Soldier Boy; OR, TOM SOMERS IN THE ARMY.
2. The Sailor Boy; OR, JACK SOMERS IN THE NAVY.
3. The Young Lieutenant; OR, ADVENTURES OF AN ARMY OFFICER.
4. The Yankee Middy; OR, ADVENTURES OF A NAVY OFFICER.
5. Fighting Joe; OR, THE FORTUNES OF A STAFF OFFICER.
6. Brave Old Salt; OR, LIFE ON THE QUARTER DECK.

"This series of six volumes recounts the adventures of two brothers, Tom and Jack Somers, one in the army, the other in the navy, in the great Civil War. The romantic narratives of the fortunes and exploits of the brothers are thrilling in the extreme. Historical accuracy in the recital of the great events of that period is strictly followed, and the result is, not only a library of entertaining volumes, but also the best history of the Civil War for young people ever written."

Boat Builders Series. By OLIVER OPTIC. In six volumes. Illustrated. Any volume sold separately. Price per volume, $1.25.

1. All Adrift; OR, THE GOLDWING CLUB.
2. Snug Harbor; OR, THE CHAMPLAIN MECHANICS.
3. Square and Compasses; OR, BUILDING THE HOUSE.
4. Stem to Stern; OR, BUILDING THE BOAT.
5. All Taut; OR, RIGGING THE BOAT.
6. Ready About; OR, SAILING THE BOAT.

"The series includes in six successive volumes the whole art of boat building, boat rigging, boat managing, and practical hints to make the ownership of a boat pay. A great deal of useful information is given in this Boat Builders Series, and in each book a very interesting story is interwoven with the information. Every reader will be interested at once in Dory, the hero of 'All Adrift,' and one of the characters retained in the subsequent volumes of the series. His friends will not want to lose sight of him, and every boy who makes his acquaintance in 'All Adrift' will become his friend."

Riverdale Story Books. By OLIVER OPTIC. Twelve volumes. Illustrated. Illuminated covers. Price: cloth, per set, $3.60; per volume, 30 cents; paper, per set, $2.00.

1. Little Merchant.	7. Proud and Lazy.
2. Young Voyagers.	8. Careless Kate.
3. Christmas Gift.	9. Robinson Crusoe, Jr.
4. Dolly and I.	10. The Picnic Party.
5. Uncle Ben.	11. The Gold Thimble.
6. Birthday Party.	12. The Do-Somethings.

Riverdale Story Books. By OLIVER OPTIC. Six volumes. Illustrated. Fancy cloth and colors. Price per volume, 30 cents.

1. Little Merchant.	4. Careless Kate.
2. Proud and Lazy.	5. Dolly and I.
3. Young Voyagers.	6. Robinson Crusoe, Jr.

Flora Lee Library. By OLIVER OPTIC. Six volumes. Illustrated. Fancy cloth and colors. Price per volume, 30 cents.

1. The Picnic Party.	4. Christmas Gift.
2. The Gold Thimble.	5. Uncle Ben.
3. The Do-Somethings.	6. Birthday Party.

These are bright short stories for younger children who are unable to comprehend the Starry Flag Series or the Army and Navy Series. But they all display the author's talent for pleasing and interesting the little folks. They are all fresh and original, preaching no sermons, but inculcating good lessons.

OLIVER OPTIC'S BOOKS

The Way of the World. By OLIVER OPTIC. Illustrated. $1.50.

"One of the most interesting American novels we have ever read." — *Philadelphia City Item.*

"This story treats of a fortune of three million dollars left a youthful heir. The volume bears evidence in every chapter of the fresh, original, and fascinating style which has always enlivened Mr. ADAMS' productions. We have the same felicitous manner of working out the plot by conversation, the same quaint wit and humor, and a class of characters which stand out boldly, pen photographs of living beings.

"The book furnishes a most romantic and withal a most instructive illustration of the way of the world in its false estimate of money."

Living too Fast; OR, THE CONFESSIONS OF A BANK OFFICER. By OLIVER OPTIC. Illustrated. $1.50.

This story records the experience of a bank officer in the downward career of crime. The career ought, perhaps, to have ended in the State's prison; but the author chose to represent the defaulter as sharply punished in another way. The book contains a most valuable lesson; and shows, in another leading character, the true life which a young business man ought to lead.

In Doors and Out; OR, VIEWS FROM A CHIMNEY CORNER. By OLIVER OPTIC. Illustrated. $1.50.

"Many who have not time and patience to wade through a long story will find here many pithy and sprightly tales, each sharply hitting some social absurdity or social vice. We recommend the book heartily after having read the three chapters on 'Taking a Newspaper.' If all the rest are as sensible and interesting as these, and doubtless they are, the book is well worthy of patronage." — *Vermont Record.*

"As a writer of domestic stories, Mr. WILLIAM T. ADAMS (OLIVER OPTIC) made his mark even before he became so immensely popular through his splendid books for the young. In the volume before us are given several of these tales, and they comprise a book which will give them a popularity greater than they have ever before enjoyed. They are written in a spirited style, impart valuable practical lessons, and are of the most lively interest." — *Boston Home Journal.*

Our Standard Bearer. A Life of Gen. U. S. Grant. By OLIVER OPTIC. Illustrated by THOMAS NAST. Illuminated covers, $1.50.

It has long been out of print, but now comes out in a new edition, with a narrative of the civil career of the General as President for two terms, his remarkable journey abroad, his life in New York, and his sickness, death, and burial. Perhaps the reader will remember that the narrative is told by "Captain Galligasken" after a style that is certainly not common or tiresome, but, rather, in a direct, simple, picturesque, and inspiring way that wins the heart of the young reader. For the boy who wants to read the life of General Grant, this book is the best that has been published,—perhaps the only one that is worth any consideration.

Just His Luck. By OLIVER OPTIC. Illustrated. $1.00.

"It deals with real flesh and blood boys; with boys who possess many noble qualities of mind; with boys of generous impulses and large hearts; with boys who delight in playing pranks, and who are ever ready for any sort of mischief; and with boys in whom human nature is strongly engrafted. They are boys, as many of us have been; boys in the true, unvarnished sense of the word; boys with hopes, ideas, and inspirations, but lacking in judgment, self-control, and discipline. And the book contains an appropriate moral, teaches many a lesson, and presents many a precept worthy of being followed. It is a capital book for boys."

J. T. TROWBRIDGE'S BOOKS

THE TIDE-MILL STORIES. 6 volumes.

Phil and His Friends. By J. T. TROWBRIDGE. Illustrated. $1.25.

The hero is the son of a man who from drink got into debt, and, after having given a paper to a creditor authorizing him to keep the son as a security for his claim, ran away, leaving poor Phil a bond slave. The story involves a great many unexpected incidents, some of which are painful, and some comic. Phil manfully works for a year, cancelling his father's debt, and then escapes. The characters are strongly drawn, and the story is absorbingly interesting.

The Tinkham Brothers' Tide-Mill. By J. T. TROWBRIDGE. Illustrated. $1.25.

"The Tinkham Brothers" were the devoted sons of an invalid mother. The story tells how they purchased a tide-mill, which afterwards, by the ill-will and obstinacy of neighbors, became a source of much trouble to them. It tells also how, by discretion and the exercise of a peaceable spirit, they at last overcame all difficulties.

"Mr. TROWBRIDGE's humor, his fidelity to nature, and story-telling power lose nothing with years; and he stands at the head of those who are furnishing a literature for the young, clean and sweet in tone, and always of interest and value." — *The Continent*.

The Satin-wood Box. By J. T. TROWBRIDGE. Illustrated. $1.25.

"Mr. TROWBRIDGE has always a purpose in his writings, and this time he has undertaken to show how very near an innocent boy can come to the guilty edge and yet be able by fortunate circumstances to rid himself of all suspicion of evil. There is something winsome about the hero; but he has a singular way of falling into bad luck, although the careful reader will never feel the least disposed to doubt his honesty. . . . . It is the pain and perplexity which impart to the story its intense interest." — *Syracuse Standard*.

The Little Master. By J. T. TROWBRIDGE. Illustrated. $1.25.

This is the story of a schoolmaster, his trials, disappointments, and final victory. It will recall to many a man his experience in teaching pupils, and in managing their opinionated and self-willed parents. The story has the charm which is always found in Mr. TROWBRIDGE's works.

"Many a teacher could profit by reading of this plucky little schoolmaster." — *Journal of Education*.

His One Fault. By J. T. TROWBRIDGE. Illustrated. $1.25.

"As for the hero of this story, 'His One Fault' was absent-mindedness. He forgot to lock his uncle's stable door, and the horse was stolen. In seeking to recover the stolen horse, he unintentionally stole another. In trying to restore the wrong horse to his rightful owner, he was himself arrested. After no end of comic and dolorous adventures, he surmounted all his misfortunes by downright pluck and genuine good feeling. It is a noble contribution to juvenile literature." — *Woman's Journal*.

Peter Budstone. By J. T. TROWBRIDGE. Illustrated. $1.25.

"TROWBRIDGE's other books have been admirable and deservedly popular, but this one, in our opinion, is the best yet. It is a story at once spirited and touching, with a certain dramatic and artistic quality that appeals to the literary sense as well as to the story-loving appetite. In it Mr. TROWBRIDGE has not lectured or moralized or remonstrated; he has simply shown boys what they are doing when they contemplate hazing. By a good artistic impulse we are not shown the hazing at all; when the story begins, the hazing is already over, and we are introduced immediately to the results. It is an artistic touch also that the boy injured is not hurt because he is a fellow of delicate nerves, but because of his very strength, and the power with which he resisted until overcome by numbers, and subjected to treatment which left him insane. His insanity takes the form of harmless delusion, and the absurdity of his ways and talk enables the author to lighten the sombreness without weakening the moral, in a way that ought to win all boys to his side." — *The Critic*.

J. T. TROWBRIDGE'S BOOKS

J. T. TROWBRIDGE'S BOOKS

THE TOBY TRAFFORD SERIES. 3 volumes.

The Fortunes of Toby Trafford. By J. T. TROWBRIDGE. Illustrated. $1.25.

"If to make children's stories as true to nature as the stories which the masters of fiction write for children of a larger growth be an uncommon achievement, and one that is worthy of wide recognition, that recognition should be given to Mr. J. T. TROWBRIDGE for his many achievements in this difficult walk of literary art. Mr. TROWBRIDGE has a good perception of character, which he draws with skill; he has abundance of invention, which he never abuses; and he has, what so many American writers have not, an easy, graceful style, which can be humorous, or pathetic, or poetic." — *R. H. Stoddard in New York Mail*.

Father Brighthopes: AN OLD CLERGYMAN'S VACATION. By J. T. TROWBRIDGE. Illustrated. $1.25.

This book was published in the early fifties by Phillips, Sampson & Co., of which firm Mr. Lee (of Lee and Shepard) was then a member. It was very favorably received, and was followed by other stories, — a long series of them, — still lengthening, and which, it is hoped, may be prolonged indefinitely. Recently a new edition has appeared, and for a preface the author has related with touching simplicity the account of his first experience in authorship.

It is well known that Mr. TROWBRIDGE is primarily a poet. Some beautiful poems of his were printed in the early numbers of the *Atlantic Monthly* (in company with poems by LONGFELLOW, EMERSON, LOWELL, and HOLMES), and were well received. "At Sea" is a gem that has become classic. The poetic faculty has not been without use to the story-writer. The perception of beauty in nature and in human nature is always evident even in his realistic prose. But his poetic gift never leads him into sentimentality, and his characters are true children of men, with natural faults as well as natural gifts and graces. His stories are intensely *human*, with a solid basis, and with an instinctive dramatic action. He has never written an uninteresting book.

Woodie Thorpe's Pilgrimage, AND OTHER STORIES. By J. T. TROWBRIDGE. Illustrated. $1.25.

"The scenes are full of human interest and lifelikeness, and will please many an old reader, as well as the younger folks for whose delectation it is intended. As in all the books of this author the spirit is manly, sincere, and in the best sense moral There is no 'goody' talk and no cant, but principles of truthfulness, integrity, and self-reliance are quietly inculcated by example. It is safe to say that any boy will be the better for reading books like this." — *St. Botolph*.

Neighbors' Wives. By J. T. TROWBRIDGE. Cloth. $1.50.

As a novelty, the following acrostic is presented. The praise from the different newspapers is brief, but to the point.

N ot in the least tiresome. — *Troy Press*.
E xquisite touches of character. — *Salem Observer*.
I ntroducing strong scenes with rare skill. — *Gloucester Telegraph*.
G roups well certain phases of character. — *New Bedford Standard*.
H appy sprightliness of style and vivacity which fascinates — *Dover Legion*.
B y many considered the author's best. — *Journal*.
O ne of the best of TROWBRIDGE's stories. — *Commonwealth*.
R eader finds it difficult to close the book. — *Hearth and Home*.
S toryall alive with adventures and incidents striking and vivid. — *Dover Star*.

W hich is one of TROWBRIDGE's brightest and best. — *Boston Transcript*.
I s destined to be enjoyed mightily. — *Salem Observer*.
V ery pleasant reading. — *New York Leader*.
E xcels any of the author's former books. — *Montana American*.
S tory is in the author's best vein. — *New Haven Register*.